Visible, yet Hidden

Crawdad Beach Series (Book 1)

Lisa Buffaloe

Visible, yet Hidden
John 15:11 Publications
Copyright 2023 Lisa Brewer Buffaloe
All rights reserved.

Visit the author's website at https://lisabuffaloe.com.

ISBN: 978-1-957715-13-1 (eBook)
ISBN: 978-1-957715-14-8 (Paperback)
ISBN: 978-1-957715-15-5 (Hardcover)
Cover design: Lisa Buffaloe.
Original photo of woman by Leeloo The First.
Crawdad illustrations: Jack Foster, https://www.jackfosterart.com

Printed in the United States of America

Visible, yet Hidden
A brutal murder. A life in hiding.
Hearts at risk.

Taken into protective custody after witnessing the murder of a drug kingpin, Marie Delgado finds herself in the quirky, small town of Crawdad Beach. Haunted by the past, can she risk her heart and her life to trust God with her future?

David Mitchell had everything most people wanted – a great family, a good job, and a hometown he loved, but one thing remained missing. When he meets Marie, is she the answer to his prayers, or will her past kill both of their hopes and dreams?

Table of Contents

Chapter 1

Resilient. She chuckled to herself. With all she'd gone through, the word resilient should be on her forehead. No matter what came her way, she kept bouncing back.

Morning sun warming her shoulders, she strolled to her favorite coffee shop. With her promotion last week, she'd been given a raise, and her picture featured in the paper. Plus, with the extra money, she'd bought a new couch and fun accessories for her apartment. Things were finally going her way.

Stepping inside the building, she took a deep breath. The scent of coffee and freshly baked pastries welcomed her as she passed tables filled with customers.

Taking her place in the long line, she stood behind a well-dressed man flanked by two massive, muscular men. The hair on the back of her neck raised. Both big men had snake tattoos curling down their arms. In her old neighborhood, those were the marks of one of the biggest drug cartels in the area.

She might be a black belt, but taking on someone like those men would not be in her best interest. Hopefully, they were only in line for coffee. Fighting was an option, but avoiding a fight was preferable.

Taking a step back, she smushed against a stocky, older

man. He scowled at her with a don't mess with me look and mumbled a curse under his breath.

Facing forward again, she readjusted her stance to keep a little distance between the men standing in front of her.

Screams split the air. Jolting, she turned as a dark-haired man with a pistol rushed toward them and raised his weapon. "You'll die for what happened to my family!"

Cursing, the tattooed men drew guns, knocking her aside.

Shots blasted around her. Glass shattered. Tables knocked over as screaming people dove for cover.

Ears ringing, she fell to the floor.

Covered in blood, the well-dressed man crumpled next to her.

Chapter 2

Thirteen months later...

Gulping air, she rushed inside her apartment and bolted the door. Although her name had been changed, her appearance altered, her long, dark hair cut short, and her gray eyes covered in brown contacts, he'd still found her.

Racing to her closet, she popped open the hidden compartment, grabbed the burner phone, and placed the dreaded call to her handler. Mr. Smith calmly reminded her what to do and how to proceed. Time was of the essence.

Hurrying, she shredded her photo work badge along with personal papers. When finished, she stuffed the phone into the back pocket of her jeans, grabbed her go-bag, Abuela's Bible, her photo album, a novel she'd bought at a thrift store, and took one final look at the apartment she'd lived in for the last thirteen months. What little she'd accumulated would be removed and destroyed. All traces of her life in apartment 3D, even her items at her work desk, would soon be gone. Nothing personal would remain.

All her life, she'd wanted to live somewhere safe, but nothing turned out as she'd hoped. Shutting down the longing within her, she took a deep breath. Her grandmother told her to give everything to God, be resilient, and, no matter what life threw her way to keep on keeping on.

She straightened her back. She could take care of herself. No way she'd live in fear. She was tough, and whatever came against her, she would be resilient. After a final inspection of the apartment, she hurried outside.

A black SUV with tinted windows waited in the parking lot. Checking first to make sure the license plate matched the numbers Mr. Smith had given her, she climbed in the back seat and threw her bag on the floorboard.

As the vehicle pulled away, she stole one final glance out the back window at another life left behind. Her car would be taken away, her employer given a cover story, and her existence erased for the second time.

The male driver maneuvered the SUV onto the freeway and weaved among traffic as they headed west. Was she being returned to California, where she first started?

The driver took the next exit and turned the vehicle east. "I needed to make sure we weren't followed," the man said.

Unable to speak at the moment, she nodded. *Get a grip.* Getting sentimental was a sign of weakness.

From the rear-view mirror, the driver surveyed her. "Just let me know when you need to make a stop. You can call me..." he cleared his throat, "Joshua."

She raised an eyebrow. For his protection, perhaps even for hers, he would remain anonymous. "Thank you, Mr. Joshua. You taking me to the promised land?"

He let out a deep chuckle, stopped at a stoplight, and turned toward her. "I'm not sure of your final destination." He looked mid-forties, with blue eyes, tanned skin, and dark hair. A jagged scar ran along the side of his face.

She'd learned to watch and make a note of anything unusual in her surroundings. That's how she'd seen the guy following her today.

As Joshua merged the vehicle onto the freeway traffic, she looked out the window. Her life had changed when she witnessed the murder. Not just any murder but one that made worldwide headlines and forever put a target on her back. She'd seen the killer, looked right into his black eyes as he pointed the gun toward them. Fortunately, she'd been knocked out of the way as bullets ripped past her head into the drug kingpin's body.

After she'd given her statement to the police, she'd been taken by Mr. Smith's team outside the police station and whisked away for her protection. She'd only been able to grab a few items before they transferred her from California to New Mexico. And now? She had no clue what was next.

She rubbed her forehead and glanced at the driver. "So, where are we going?"

Joshua kept his eyes on the road. "We'll stay tonight at a hotel a few states from here. When we check in, I'll stay in the room next to yours. In the morning, another driver will take over for the next part of your journey. Mr. Smith wants to make sure you're safe."

Her driver's answer wasn't really an answer, but at least Mr. Smith knew where she was going. "Have you ever met Mr. Smith? I've only talked to him on the phone." She'd only heard his voice, deep, soothing, and steady.

Joshua gazed at her through the rear-view mirror. "Mr. Smith's a great guy. He takes care of those who are his. I've known him for years. He's taken many people under his wing."

"Did he take care of you?"

Joshua didn't say anything for a moment. "We all have our stories." He ran his hand along his scar. "Some just draw more attention than others. By the way, your name is now Marie Delgado. When we stop for the night, a packet will be waiting with the information you need."

Marie Delgado. Marie Delgado. She repeated the name in her mind, trying to make sure she could remember who she was this time.

"Hey, you'll be okay." Joshua's deep voice interrupted her thoughts. "Sometimes, when life takes a different direction, we think it's not good, but a new door only opens when an old door closes. Plus, the road gets boring without bumps and turns."

"I think I'd like boring for a while." She hated the thought of starting again, another new name, a new place, always the outcast, constantly looking over her shoulder, wondering if she would be found.

"Hey, I'm sorry. I know this isn't easy. I'm not making light of the situation. We're doing everything possible to ensure your safety. It's a long, monotonous drive ahead, so just let me know when you need a stop. You can sit up front when we get further down the road." Joshua glanced over his shoulder. "If you want to talk, I'm a good listener."

"Thanks. I'll just rest for a while. I will take you up later on the front seat." Marie turned to survey the barren landscape. With the arrival of Spring, the flat fields were finally green. Farm and cattle land stretched before them. A herd of cows stood in a pasture under a lone oak tree.

Marie sighed. *Alone again.* Why couldn't she get a break? Closing her eyes, she tried to rest.

Four hours later, after a quick stop for gas and a restroom break, Marie buckled in the front seat and turned to her driver. "Have you done this kind of thing before?"

Joshua pulled the SUV back onto the open road. "A few times." His jacket moved as he turned the wheel, exposing a holster and gun.

"Ever had anything happen?" She pointed toward his gun. "Any excitement?"

"I've had some. But don't worry, I have a feeling this trip will be without any drama."

"I could use some non-dramatic days." She'd prefer some quiet decades. She hated drama of any kind.

"We can hope for that." Joshua nodded. "I'll pray for you too."

Marie surveyed him for a moment before looking out the front window. He didn't look like the praying type, more like the bash-your-head-in type.

"My Abuela used to pray."

"Abuela? Oh, you mean your grandmother. She sounds like a good woman."

"Yes, I still miss her. But that's life, mostly bad with some good sprinkled in along the way."

Joshua's gaze seemed to hold compassion as he glanced her way. "Maybe this move will give you the opportunity for more good than bad."

"That'd be nice. I'm not holding my breath, but it would be nice." Marie leaned back on the headrest. She didn't know what else to say or how to keep a conversation going when she wasn't supposed to ask questions or share too much information. Would there ever be a time when she could just talk with people, relax, not worry who was listening, and just be herself? Then again, she didn't even know who she was anymore.

Not that she ever had a clear identity anyway. She'd been raised in a small two-bedroom rental house in a part of the city most people avoided. Marie rubbed at the faint burn scar on her arm, the reminder of the car wreck that killed her parents when she was a baby. Only she had survived.

The few photos of her parents showed Marie's mom had a beautiful exotic look, with long black hair and tanned skin, a mixture of Asian and Spanish descent. Her dad was also bi-racial, a mix of black and white, with grey eyes, tall, light chocolate skin tone, a well-built, good-looking military man.

Abuela told her they'd been sweet people with a wonderful marriage who deeply loved one another and loved her. Then she'd hug Marie and tell her she was a perfect blend of the races, the best of the world.

Marie disagreed. With her mixed race, she never fit in any group. Her skin was too light for some and too dark for others. Her gray eye color was wrong for some races; others found them fascinating – mainly dirty old men who frequented the retail stores where she worked during high school and college.

Why people judged anyone based on race was beyond

her. It didn't make sense to think any group of people were superior or better than another.

Maybe becoming Marie Delgado would allow her to blend in wherever they placed her next. Either way, she would be resilient. She would survive.

Closing her eyes, she tried to stop her thoughts. Sleep gave a way to avoid worrying about the future. Sometimes, she dreamed of living somewhere safe, having a loving family and a home. Other times, nightmares would invade. If only she could program the dreams she wanted.

She jolted awake. The SUV had stopped. Surprised she'd slept, she rubbed at the crick in her neck and stared at the night sky. Not one dream, not one nightmare. She must have been more tired than she thought.

"We'll stay here tonight." Joshua turned off the interior light before stepping out of the vehicle. "Keep the doors locked while I check in."

When he returned, darkness shielded their entrance into the hotel's side entrance. At the room, Marie stepped aside as Joshua ensured there were no hidden cameras or listening devices.

"All clear." He waited as she entered. "I'll be in the room next to you. Keep the connecting door locked on your side. Mine will remain unlocked if you need anything. We'll leave at six in the morning. I hope you can sleep well."

She shrugged. "I'll try."

Joshua stopped and turned her way. "I know this isn't easy. Tomorrow will be a new day with a new beginning."

Marie thanked him, locked the door, and then plopped

on the double bed. A new beginning sounded good in theory but leaving behind everything again stunk. Why couldn't she have family, friends, and a place to belong?

Her grandmother had loved and treated her well, but growing up in their neighborhood was more than difficult. The courses she'd taken in self-defense and martial arts had come in handy far too often.

Marie rechecked the hotel door locks and opened the packet waiting for her. The contents included her latest cover story, a new driver's license and credit card in her new name, a high-security phone already programmed with Mr. Smith's number, and a copy of her college transcript she'd attended on scholarship also with her new name.

A canvas bag contained several outfits, a light jacket, and shoes. How Mr. Smith, or whoever was keeping an eye on her, knew her size was beyond her. Thankfully, she could purchase whatever else was needed with her new credit card.

Marie took out Abuela's Bible and held it close to her chest. Even if they couldn't be together, at least she had her grandmother's most treasured possession. Opening the book, the pages fell to chapter forty-three in Isaiah. The verses were about not remembering past events because God was about to do something new, that he would make a way in the wilderness and streams in the desert.

Was she being warned she'd wind up in a wilderness or a desert? Maybe they were driving her east to an airport to fly her to the Sahara. That would be just her luck.

She looked again at the Bible verses. Then again, maybe this time, the new place would be positive. She was ready to start fresh. Placing the Bible beside her, she threw the covers over her head and tried to sleep.

Bolting up in bed, Marie tried to get her bearings. Recognition slowly crept into her brain. She was somewhere in a hotel with a guy next door, supposedly named Joshua, taking her on a journey to somewhere.

The bedside clock showed five a.m. Too awake to get back to sleep, she stumbled to the shower to prepare for the next part of her travels to who knew where.

At six o'clock, a tap sounded. "You awake?" Joshua's voice carried through the closed door.

Ready for the day, Marie let him inside.

He handed her a breakfast biscuit and a cup of coffee. "Ms. Joshua is waiting out front. I'll escort you to her car."

"Ms. Joshua? Any relation?"

"No. She's much tougher than I am." He gave her a slight grin, then stopped and turned to her, his expression serious. "I'll be praying for you. We might not like the difficult roads we travel, but God promises that all things work for the good for those who love him and are called to his purpose. You've got a calling on your life, so trust God, and as much as you can, try to enjoy the journey." He turned and continued walking beside her to the parking lot.

When she was growing up, her grandmother had told her something similar. But right now, even if everything worked out, how could she enjoy the journey when someone was still trying to kill her?

A lean woman, around her mid-forties, her black hair pulled back in a ponytail, stood beside another dark SUV.

After thanking and saying goodbye to Joshua, Marie jumped in the car with the new driver.

Ms. Joshua's head tilted as she studied Marie, then gave her a brief smile. "Make yourself comfortable and tell me when you need a stop."

Since there didn't seem to be an option for talking, Marie settled in her seat, ate her biscuit, and finished her coffee.

Fortunately, she had brought a mystery novel and was already on the fourth book of a six-part series. Despite being shot at as she chased a killer across the country, the main character remained unfazed. She was tough, intelligent, and had a great sense of humor. Marie imagined herself in the role since she didn't want to be like the wimpy women who cried over the least little problem. Even though life was hard, she would be tough and resilient.

Deep into the book's story, Marie returned to reality as the car slowed.

Ms. Joshua parked the vehicle at an abandoned gas station next to an older light grey car and then turned to face her. "The keys are under the side passenger mat. You'll receive directions to where you're going." She smiled. "Enjoy the new story of your life."

Marie thanked her, stepped out, and stretched the stiffness from her back. Being shipped across the country to some unknown destination wasn't her idea of enjoyable. She settled into her new car, surprised that the interior was immaculate and still had a new car smell.

Her phone alerted her of an incoming text. Mr. Smith sent her the address to her next location and finished with,

"Enjoy your new place and your new life."

Enjoy? Why did everyone tell her to enjoy? How could she do that with a killer still on the loose? Abuela told her not to dwell on the past but instead look to the future and trust that God had a plan for her. She would also remind her that no matter how others behaved, she could choose how she lived.

Marie shook her head. Her only current option was following directions wherever Mr. Smith sent her. The GPS showed she still had over an hour before she reached her next stop. Marie buckled in and drove along a pine tree-lined country road. Every few miles, blacktop or gravel driveways led to houses and farms of various sizes.

Forty-five minutes into her journey, the road crossed under an interstate leading to a popular beach town. A bank, pharmacy, fast food place, hotel, and one of those huge all-in-one stores graced the intersection. A sign to the right pointed to an industrial park.

Traffic remained light as Marie continued driving down the two-lane road. She crossed a bridge over an inlet waterway that looked to be no more than a small sandy river. A sign directed people to visit Wilderness State Park.

She slammed on her brakes. She knew it. She'd been shipped to the wilderness.

Chapter 3

What would he do with 288 cans of tomato sauce? David Mitchell rubbed the back of his neck. "I ordered two dozen cans, not twenty-four dozen."

The delivery guy shrugged his shoulders. "I just bring what they tell me to bring."

"I know it's not your fault." David checked the invoice and noticed the significant discount the store would receive for this quantity. "I'll figure out something. Thanks for your help." He signed the paperwork and looked around the already crowded stockroom. They could keep more items if they were bigger, but space was always limited. Life in a small town restricted what they could sell and stock.

Fortunately, the local organic produce and meat they offered kept customers coming from miles around. As for the extra cans, he'd set up a display with recipes that needed tomato sauce. His nephews and nieces could eat spaghetti every day.

David went to his office in the back, inputted the items from the invoice, and checked how the store was doing. So far this month, they were making a decent profit. Creativity was the key. Running specials for customers kept their little store profitable.

He did a quick search on his favorite cooking websites.

Using his graphic design skills, he printed various recipes on card stock. Hopefully, people would buy the cans and all the ingredients they needed.

Growing up, he couldn't wait to escape Crawdad Beach, South Carolina. As a kid, he thought he'd live in Europe, but instead, here he was working in the family business at Mitchells' Grocery Store. Life was funny that way. First, he'd gone away to attend university on a baseball scholarship but broke his wrist. Then, his college girlfriend decided she preferred someone else.

After graduation, he'd traveled across Europe. The life he'd lived abroad still made him cringe. He felt ashamed of his behavior overseas and took a job in Chicago. However, he soon realized that his boyhood dreams of living far away from his hometown and family were not what he wanted. Fortunately, God and his family were forgiving.

David arranged the stack of recipe cards on a display to attract shoppers. He smiled as he looked around the store. The hours were often long, but he loved his job and visiting with people.

The slower pace in Crawdad Beach was nice, but a little excitement would be welcome. The town had a few single women, but not many. The older ladies in the area kept trying to set him up with their daughters or granddaughters. And the women he'd met online didn't want to live in a small town or were nothing like their profiles. He could write a book on his many disastrous dates.

God knew his desires. Not that he was deserving, but since he was twenty-seven, he was ready to be married like all his siblings. He'd love a wife, preferably someone intelligent, with a great sense of humor, good-looking, a Christian, who would fit into his fun and unique family. However, at the rate things were going, God would have to parachute her into their small town.

Chapter 4

A cartoon crawdad? Marie stopped at a blinking red light and stared at a sign with a cute crawfish welcoming people to Crawdad Beach. A gas station with a small convenience store stood on one corner of the street. Across from it was a volunteer fire department next to a large white-steepled church.

Crossing a railroad track with weeds growing between the rails, she noticed a public library in what looked like the old railroad station. The side of the building had a mural painted of a cute cartoon crawdad sitting on a beach reading a book.

Marie drove slowly down the brick-paved main street. Cars were parked in front of most of the two-story brick buildings, many of which had flower-lined balconies on their second floors. Although some buildings appeared unoccupied, they were still neatly maintained. One of the buildings had been converted into loft apartments, and another was being renovated. Several others functioned as a law office, post office, the Knick Knacks Antique store, the Curl and Dye Beauty Salon, and Tiddlywinks Restaurant.

A young woman dressed in jogging gear pushed a stroller along the sidewalk, and an elderly couple walked their little white dog.

A nice-looking middle-aged, dark-skinned gentleman wearing a teal polo shirt and khaki shorts smiled and waved as Marie drove past.

She slowed in front of Doohickeys Hardware to read their sign. Since 1916, they proudly offered a wide range of hardware, building supplies, and whatever whatchamacallit needed. She grinned. That was her kind of store.

Marie stepped on her brakes. *Where on earth had Mr. Smith sent her?* A woman, wearing a bright pink velveteen jogging suit, hunched over the wheel of a riding lawnmower as though street racing. She even had a pink basket tied to the back of the seat. At least the town seemed to have a sense of humor.

Beyond the shops of Main Street stood several stately, distinguished houses, two-story Victorians, a red-brick colonial house with white columns, craftsman-type cottages, and bungalows.

The road curved around a community park. Curious, Marie stopped in the parking lot and hopped out of her car. She stood inhaling the sweet scent of blooming flowers and listened to the leaves flutter in the light breeze. The historical marker revealed the town, established in 1881, received the name from one of the children who had noticed a crawdad sunning himself on the small sandy riverbank.

Peaceful serenity of blooming crepe myrtles, pine trees, and a giant oak with moss hanging from its branches surrounded her as she surveyed the little park. A play area for kids, wooden benches, and a sidewalk meandered next to the riverbank. Crawdad Beach just might be a good place to start over.

Back in her car, she continued exploring. She rested her arm in the open window, letting the sun warm her and the wind whip through her short hair.

Satisfied she'd checked out the area, she stopped at the end of a cul-de-sac in front of a duplex that would be her new residence. Marie leaned over her steering wheel and scanned the place Mr. Smith had sent her. White shutters and doors provided a clean and crisp contrast to the sea-green building, giving it a classic, timeless appearance. Each unit even had garages. Mature landscaping with a mix of flowers and plants added color and beauty to the exterior of the building.

As she exited her car, the door to the right side duplex opened, and a couple walked toward her. A woman, around her late forties, with sandy brown hair and eyes, stopped before her and smiled. "You must be Marie."

At Marie's nod, she continued. "I'm Julie Bowman. Welcome to Crawdad Beach and your new home. This is my husband, Dustin."

The man with dark hair and blue eyes smiled. "We're glad you're here. Come on, and we'll show you around."

Dustin unlocked the door to the unit on the left, handed her the key, and led her inside. "The house is fully furnished."

Marie followed the couple into an immaculate, open living area with light blue walls and plank wood vinyl flooring. A soft white couch, two brightly colored floral chairs, a coffee table, and a flat-screen television perched on a white cabinet made up the furniture. The rear of the room contained the kitchen and dining area. Light streamed in from glass French doors at the back.

"We're a small family town with mostly blue-collar neighborhoods." Dustin talked as she surveyed the room. "The town isn't really on the beach. The ocean is about forty-five minutes from here. If you like being outdoors, you've moved to the right place. We're surrounded by natural beauty, with nearby forests, wetlands, and waterways offering opportunities for outdoor recreation such as hiking, hunting, boating, and fishing. Many people here are retired, work in the small shops and area industries, or commute to bigger cities. The freeway bypassed us, but no matter what comes against Crawdad Beach, we will keep on keeping on. Plus, those difficulties allowed us to build a quiet life for the residents."

Marie smiled at the man. If the town could keep on keeping on, so could she.

Julie nudged her husband. "Dustin, she's already going to live here. You don't need to give her your sales pitch." She gave Marie an apologetic smile. "Don't mind him. He's the town mayor when he's not working at his company."

Dustin nodded. "She's a lawyer if you ever have any legal questions. Your realtor, Mr. Smith, was great to work with. He wired money and emailed a list of things to get for you, so Julie stocked the essentials."

"That's very kind of him and you both. Thank you." Marie couldn't believe how Mr. Smith continued to take care of her. What he did seemed far beyond what was usually done for someone in protective custody.

"Truly extraordinary," Julie echoed her thoughts. "We've

never talked to anyone like him. Oh, and you're paid up for the next twelve months. We're excited to have someone like you renting our place."

Twelve months already paid, and her place stocked with essentials? Mr. Smith had really gone overboard this time. Marie gave Julie a pleasant smile. If only the lady knew why she was moving here, she probably wouldn't be quite so enthusiastic.

Julie showed her the white-cabinet kitchen and dining area with a round, white-washed wooden table with four chairs. "We have a local grocery store for anything else you might need. Let me show you the bedroom and bathroom. I hope you like everything. With Mr. Smith's money, I could also get all new linens."

Dustin followed the women. "Julie has had a blast getting it ready for you."

Julie grinned and nodded. "I must admit I did enjoy myself. Everything is washed and ready to go. You should just be able to unpack and settle in." Julie guided Marie to the bedroom decorated with a light teal bedspread and rattan furniture, with white shutter shades covering the windows. Even the bathroom shower curtain had a beach scene.

Dustin met them in the hallway. "The garage is through the laundry area. You have a stackable washer and dryer. You'll be able to park and shut the garage. It keeps you out of the rain and keeps things private. I left the remote opener on the kitchen counter for you. We also have a security system, cable, and Wi-Fi. I'll show you how to set everything before we go."

Julie smiled at her husband. "When Dustin isn't doing his mayor thing, he works in software security, so he knows his stuff. We also left our number if you need anything." She motioned toward the rear of the house. "I put a few potted plants for you on the back porch. I think plants always make things homier."

She led Marie to the screened-in covered patio with vibrant flowers spilling out of brightly colored pots. "Beyond our backyard is the home of the Taylors. They're a sweet, older couple who've lived in the area for over fifty years. I'll have to introduce you once you get settled."

"Feel free to explore the town," Dustin said. "Crawdad Beach prides itself on having a safe environment for our citizens."

The couple briefed Marie on how to set up the security system, gave her the password for the Wi-Fi, and then returned to their side of the duplex.

Marie stood in the middle of her new place and surveyed each angle. Fortunately, there were few blind spots.

After unpacking her belongings, she wandered around, exploring and checking the locks on the windows and doors. The duplex welcomed her with light, security, and seemingly good neighbors. Her grandmother would have loved the place. Marie could visualize Abuela with her arms spread out, thanking Jesus for the blessing.

In honor of her grandmother, Marie paused and looked up at the ceiling. "Thank you, Jesus."

Stomach rumbling, Marie checked the kitchen for something to eat. Even though she had basic canned and boxed staples, a fresh salad sounded even better.

A few minutes later, she entered the local store and pushed a cart down the aisle. For a small business, they carried a surprising variety of items, almost like a mini farmers market with local produce, honey, jellies, and jams. Near the vegetables and produce was a display with recipe cards from people in the area. She could get used to this. Her taste buds were as varied as her mixed heritage, and it would be nice to try new things.

Marie turned down the cereal aisle and side-stepped an older couple.

"You need your bran." The woman with a white bouffant hairdo waved a cereal box at the man standing next to her.

He snatched a box off the shelf of probably the most sugary, unhealthiest of the group and grinned at the woman. "Maybelline, I've tried to live reasonably all my life. Life is too short not to live dangerously."

"Chester Taylor, what am I going to do with you?"

He moved close to the woman and nuzzled her neck. "You are going to love me forever."

The woman giggled and hugged him.

Marie grinned at the couple as they continued in good-natured banter, but inside, she wanted to cry. She missed her grandmother's hugs and so wanted someone to love her. Trying to ignore her longings, she stopped at a display for tomato sauce and examined the recipe cards free for the taking.

Cooking for one person was boring, and she needed all the help she could get. She'd lost over ten pounds since she'd been on the run. Not much for some people, but since she only stood five foot four and was already thin, she looked a touch emaciated. Not that it mattered. No one would care.

Moving on, she maneuvered around a dark-haired male employee stocking shelves in the frozen food section.

"Can I help you find something?"

"I'm just looking." Marie turned to face the store employee. He looked near her age, and his skin coloring and the shape of his dark brown eyes appeared part Asian—extremely handsome part-Asian.

He pointed to individually packaged meals in a bag. "Well, the ones made by this manufacturer are the best. They are yummy."

She raised an eyebrow at his choice of words. "Yummy?"

His face took on a red tint. "Sorry, I've been hanging around my three-year-old niece and nephew too much. Let me rephrase." He stood taller. "The food by this manufacturer is delectable and delightful."

She noted his nametag -- *David Mitchell, Store Manager*, "Thanks, David."

"You're welcome." He grinned. "Let me know if I can help with anything."

Marie nodded and pushed her cart to the next aisle. Perhaps here in Crawdad Beach, she'd be okay. Maybe Joshua had been right, and the closed door that brought her here would be an open door for a good, new beginning. Well, duh. Regardless of what happened, this would be a new beginning.

Taking her time, she examined the items on the shelves. Maybe she should buy a cookbook specializing in cooking for one person. Better yet, she could start watching cooking shows to help her think outside boxed, bagged, and canned food.

"You've got to try Mrs. Taylor's squash casserole recipe." David walked toward her. "It's great."

Marie turned to face him. "There are several recipes that sound very good."

"I've tried most of them. Or should I say, I've eaten most of them when my family has cooked them, or one of the older ladies brings me a meal." He grinned and gave a one-shoulder shrug. "I'm not much of a cook. It's not worth the effort when it's just me."

"Cooking for one person isn't much fun." She took the recipe card and pointed her cart to get the ingredients. "Maybe I'll try to make a small version of the squash recipe for myself."

David walked alongside her. "I don't mean to be nosy, but are you new to the area?"

She hesitated for a moment. "Yes, just moved here."

"Great! Welcome to Crawdad Beach. If there's anything you need, just let me know. I work most days, but we're closed on Sunday. And if you have any questions about the area, I'll gladly help." David handed her his business card with the store information. Taking a pen from his pocket, he scribbled his cell number at the bottom.

"Thank you, David." Her cheeks heated as he just stood staring at her with a big grin on his face. "I guess I need to get finished."

"Oh, right. Sorry. It's *really* great to have you here. I

mean, thanks for shopping with us." He turned and half-ran around the corner.

Marie grinned. Had David been flirting with her? The guy seemed to have a cute personality and cute humor. He even seemed to enjoy his family.

She'd been avoiding guys for years, but Mr. Smith did tell her to enjoy her life. Why would he say that unless he knew she was safe? Or, maybe he was just letting her know that regardless of what happened next, she could make the best of her time. She was ready to live, and any town with a cartoon Crawdad as a mascot couldn't be all bad.

Marie fingered David's business card. Should she call him when she returned to her place? If she did, what would she say? He didn't even know her name. If she did call him, what would be her excuse? Maybe she could ask him about a good dentist. Not that she needed one. She could ask about the local restaurant, but that would sound like she was fishing for a date. Not that she was, although that would be nice.

She picked up items to make a salad and a few other things she needed and turned toward the cashier lines. If she made a friend, what would happen if she had to leave? Still, she didn't want to be alone all her life. Goodness, her thoughts were all over the place.

Her grandmother would have told her to pray. Marie sighed. She *should* pray. She knew that deep down, but part of her was still angry with God for taking her parents and grandmother.

Running from God hadn't solved anything but made her even more lonely and alone. Maybe she'd look through

Abuela's Bible and see if another verse popped out. She could use all the help she could get.

Chapter 5

David hurried to his office. Man, he acted as if he'd never seen a woman. Okay, he'd never seen someone like her before. Her eyes held a hint of mystery, maybe even a little sadness. She was gorgeous, exotic looking, and looked about his age, and she had even moved to the area. But he didn't even know her name. *Oh, man.* And he'd acted like the desperate single guy that he was.

Maybe he could help at one of the registers, hoping she'd come his way. Would that be too obvious? Stalking someone in his store probably wouldn't be the best idea.

He needed to get back to work. Items needed to be placed on shelves, and he was always short-handed since his dad had semi-retired. His stockroom helper, associate, cashier, and all-around good guy, Tony, was off today fishing for those in the area who struggled to make ends meet.

David straightened his back. Best act like a store manager. If he was lucky, he might run into the mystery woman again. He opened the stockroom doors and screeched to a stop. Mrs. Cowman stomped toward him. With no time to escape, he pasted on what hopefully would pass as a pleasant expression.

"David." The older woman stopped and gave him her syrupy, crocodile smile. "Have you called my daughter yet?

She's been waiting for two weeks."

"No, ma'am, I'm sorry." He wouldn't give her an excuse. There was no way he wanted to take the woman's daughter on a date. In high school, her daughter made his life miserable with her rude jokes and rude proposals and then lied about him to other students, saying he had done things he would never have done. At least not while he was in high school.

Mrs. Cowman leaned closer, her dark eyes surveying him and her pungent perfume nauseating his senses. "She mentioned she would love to see you."

He backed away. "Give her my best. I need to get a few things done, excuse me." He turned and walked as fast as he could to the other side of the store. If only he had an invisibility cloak he could deploy when he wanted to disappear.

Hoping the coast was clear, he rounded the corner of the next aisle and ran headlong into the mystery woman.

She stepped back and raised an eyebrow. "Are you stalking me?"

Heat roasted his neck. "Uh...." He closed his mouth and tried not to say something crazy.

"I'm just kidding. I know you work here."

David let out a breath. "Yeah, thanks. Anything I can help you with?"

"No, I'm enjoying looking around."

David stuffed his hands in his pockets. "Would it be okay to ask your name?"

She studied him as a blush rose to her cheeks. "My name is Marie."

"That's a nice name."

Her shoulders rose in a shrug. "It's not bad, I guess."

"No, really, it's nice." David rubbed the back of his neck. Why couldn't he act semi-intelligent and stop rambling?

She looked up at him, and a small smile appeared. "Since I'm new here. Is there a dentist, a good place to eat, or anything I should know about the area?"

"A great dentist is in the next town. Dr. Griffin. You'd like him. And our local meat and three is excellent."

Her head titled. "Meat and three? That's the name of the restaurant?"

"No, that's at Tiddlywinks. You get your choice of a meat and three vegetables. The best part is they list fruit cobbler as a vegetable." He grinned and wiggled his eyebrows at her.

"Sounds yummy."

"Yeah, it's yummy." He chuckled at her response. Her big brown eyes even had a twinkle to them. "I'd gladly take you some time and introduce you to the owners."

She switched her attention away from him as her gaze traveled to the floor.

Had he made her nervous? "I'm sorry. I don't mean to make you uncomfortable."

Her smile was guarded as her gaze traveled back to his. "It's okay. I'd like to go with you."

"That's great." He knew his grin was idiotic, but he couldn't help it. "Thank you."

"I look forward to it." Her smile was shy, stunning.

"What's going on here?"

David turned as the silver-haired police chief walked

toward them. "Hey, Chief. How are you?" He shook the man's hand. "How's the family?"

"Great. Kids and grandkids are keeping me busy." He turned his attention to Marie. "So, who is this young lady?"

"This is Marie. She just moved to the area. Marie, this is Chief Weaver."

"Nice to meet you," Marie said.

"You must be the young woman staying at the Bowman place."

Her eyes rounded, her knuckles whitening where she gripped her cart. "Yes, sir."

The chief surveyed her for a moment. "I didn't catch your last name?"

"Delgado."

His eyebrows rose for a brief second, and then his eyes narrowed. "Marie Delgado. Any relation to Sam Delgado?"

She shook her head. "No, not that I know of."

"Good. Well, let me know if I can be of service." He turned to David. "Take care of yourself, tell the family hello for me, and hug those sweet kids."

"Will do, Chief." David returned his focus to Marie. Had the chief's abruptness made her nervous? She seemed worried. What if she thought the kids belonged to him?

He held up his hands. "The chief meant my family, not *my* family. They aren't my kids. I'm not married and don't have kids. I'd like to someday, but not anytime soon." Once again, he was rambling.

"It's okay." Her words said one thing, while her body language showed she was clearly uncomfortable. "I'm just not used to people knowing where I live."

"Oh, sorry. It's a small town. News travels fast. But hey, it's safe here. Well, I mean, the town's not perfect, but for the most part, people are pretty decent in these parts. So, are we still on for getting together?" At her hesitant nod, he continued. "Could I have your number?"

Her gaze studied his face. "How about we just set a day and time? Maybe meet for lunch?"

"Lunch is good. How about tomorrow at noon at Tiddlywinks Restaurant on Main Street? I could meet you there. Is that okay?"

"That would be nice. Thank you."

David stood there as she walked away. Whatever caused her to be uncomfortable, he would do his best to make her feel welcome.

That evening, David worked on his latest home improvement project. Why anyone had originally installed a pink tile backsplash with yellow and brown tile countertops was beyond him. The combination was not pretty and not appetizing.

An hour later, he felt a tug on his pant leg.

"You have to kiss it, Uncle David." Emily's big brown eyes stared at him. "Boo, boos don't heal without a kiss."

Obviously, the pink bandage he'd put on her imaginary wound wasn't enough. He leaned down and kissed the cute little finger of his three-year-old niece. "Is that better?"

Her brown curly hair bobbed with her nod. "But he has one too." Emily pointed to her twin brother.

Eric held up his hand. "I got one right here." He waved

his fingers in front of David.

"I have just what the doctor ordered." David placed a camo bandage on his nephew's finger.

Both kids thanked him, then skipped off to play in his backyard.

"You're so good with kids." David's sister, Tess, gave him a sly smile as she leaned against his kitchen cabinet. "When are you going to settle down and raise a family?"

"Easier said than done." He used a crowbar to pop off the old tile. Why couldn't remodeling be done in an hour like home improvement television shows? He'd worked on the old house for six months and had barely made a dent in the never-ending projects.

Tess helped him by cleaning off the tile shrapnel and throwing it in the garbage. "Still no luck on the dating front?"

"No. The last woman I met seemed nice, but when I met her in person, she was at least fifteen years older than me. Plus, she was scary and desperate." He shuddered. "I barely got out of the restaurant alive."

His sister chuckled. "That sounds a little dramatic."

He stopped and looked her way. "Really, sis. It was bad, *very* bad."

"Well, a good woman is out there somewhere."

David tried to remove a tile that seemed to have been stuck on the wall with cement. "Maybe I'm supposed to be a bachelor." At least, he hoped not.

"I doubt it. I picture you married with oodles of kids and grandkids one day."

"Oodles? I can't even find anyone nice to date. I don't see

that happening anytime soon."

"Have you prayed about it?"

"Yes. Well, kind of sort of. I prayed, but God knows what I really want. With all the mistakes I've made in my life, why should I be picky? It seems a little sacrilegious to talk to God about how the woman would believe, act, and look."

"Maybe you ask, and then God will surprise you with someone amazing." Tess hugged him. "I'm going to stop by Grandad's place, then get the kids home for dinner. Do you want to join us? We're having spaghetti. Your display at the grocery store was clever with all the different recipes."

"The supplier accidentally sent 288 cans, so I had to figure out something to get them out the door. Thanks for the dinner invitation, but I'll pass. I'd like to get all the old tiles removed. Then I'll crash on the couch and watch a mystery movie. A man's got to get his excitement somewhere."

She grinned as she shook her head. "Don't work too hard. I'll pass on the word to the other moms at church and daycare and try to drum up business for the store. Oh, and I'll pray about that special woman God has planned for you. She's out there somewhere."

David hugged his sister, nephew, and niece goodbye. This is one time he wished his sister would be right, that a woman was out there for him. He grinned as Marie's face came to mind. Now, she was definitely someone he could pray for.

Chapter 6

Sunrise painted the sky a brilliant orange and soft peach. Clouds resembling cotton candy floated in the gentle breeze. Marie carried a cup of coffee out on the covered screened-in patio and sat on the cushioned wicker chair. Sunlight pooled warmth across the floor.

Muted voices came from beyond the patio dividing wall between Marie's unit and the Bowmans. Although she couldn't hear their conversation clearly, she could tell it was pleasant and lighthearted. Back where she grew up, the neighbors usually shouted and cursed at one another.

After what happened at the grocery store, it had taken Marie most of the evening before settling down. The police chief hadn't seemed friendly, and how he looked at her made her uncomfortable. Maybe he didn't like her mixed race. Then again, David obviously wasn't pure white, and the chief had been very cordial with him.

She was probably just being paranoid. Hopefully, Mr. Smith researched the town before she came here. But she thought New Mexico would have been safe after they moved her from California. Hiding in a small city like Crawdad Beach seemed strange, but if someone did come looking for her, maybe blending in with the locals was the best way not to stand out.

A bird twilled in the branches of the backyard trees. Vibrant flowers bordered the manicured lawn. Never in her wildest dreams did she think she'd live in a place with so much beauty and peace.

A slight movement drew her attention to the flowers her landlords had left for her. A chameleon, blending into the surroundings, sat on the ledge of a pot and surveyed her.

Stooping down next to him, she put out her hand. "You probably need to go in the yard to find something to eat. I won't hurt you."

Closing his eyes, he ignored her offer.

Maybe, like him, she'd found a place to blend into her environment. She was almost two thousand miles away from California. No one knew her real name, she had no online identity, and no one here would know anything about her but what she chose to share.

While in New Mexico, she'd kept to herself, went to work, and secluded herself in her apartment. Outside her job, she'd spent more time being paranoid than enjoying life.

What if she genuinely embraced being Marie Delgado? There was no going back to who she was before. She went inside, put on her sunglasses, and grabbed her keys.

Forty-five minutes later, Marie stood and surveyed the Atlantic Ocean. The East Coast didn't look much different from the West. The tide ebbed and flowed, washing the shore, exposing then hiding.

Digging her bare toes into the sand, Marie sat on the beach just out of reach of the water. The sounds of the ocean refreshed and calmed her mind. A seagull glided in the morning air, dancing above the waves.

A hermit crab, his shell on his back, scurried by. He paused, seemed to glance her way, and tucked into his shell. She knew how that felt. So many times, she'd been afraid and hid from the world.

Even though she felt like she'd already lived a lifetime, she was only twenty-four. Maybe she could pretend the first part of her life was just a bad movie, and the next part would be her real life. *Why not?*

Rising to her feet, she strolled along the water's edge, letting the water tickle her toes. A tiny crab held up his pincers as though a mighty warrior. Marie chuckled as she backed away. Further up the beach, a slender white object caught her eye. She dug around, pulled out a perfectly round sand dollar, and placed it in her pocket.

After a long walk, she drove to the big store by the interstate to pick up a few items. Fortunately, she found a cute sundress and a pair of sandals for her lunch date with David.

She returned to her duplex and placed the sand dollar on the cabinet in the family room. Her first treasure for her new home. Did she dare dream she could call someplace home? Abuela had told her to plant her roots in Jesus so that wherever she went, she would always be home in Jesus. How could that be possible when God seemed so far away?

Stepping out on her patio, she checked on the chameleon. He'd moved and now clung to the screen door. Not one to be squeamish, she gently picked him up and placed him in the grass outside. Her friend looked up at her momentarily, then moved toward the patio, stopped, and jumped onto the outer screen. Her friend was here to stay. Maybe she was too.

Her phone signaled an incoming text. She glanced at a message from Mr. Smith. *"Delivery on your porch is from me."*

She ran and peeked through the front door peephole just as an unmarked white van pulled out of her driveway. A stack of large boxes sat on her porch.

After a few minutes of pushing and pulling everything inside, she used a kitchen knife to open what Mr. Smith had sent. She gasped with a part cry, part squeal. Her clothes from her last apartment, her computer, and even many of the little things she'd collected were inside. She thought they would have been destroyed, but here they were.

Her phone trilled with another incoming message from Mr. Smith, *"Hope these help you settle into your new home."*

Marie texted back her thanks, including a ton of happy face emojis. Who *was* Mr. Smith? Maybe he was her guardian angel.

If only he'd arrived sooner.

After putting her things away, she stood and looked around. Sunshine streamed through the front windows. The apartment seemed more and more like hers.

The day was too pretty to waste sitting around inside. She grabbed her house key, exited the front door, and glanced down the street.

At a house across the road, a silver-haired gentleman, holding a small garbage bag, picked up fallen magnolia leaves. A limping, little black and white dog followed close to the man.

As Marie walked in his direction, the man straightened and looked her way. He regarded her for a moment, his blue eyes piercing and radiant. "Hello. You must be new here. I'm Henry Doss."

She shook his outstretched hand. "Hello, Mr. Doss. I'm Marie Delgado."

"Ah, welcome to the neighborhood. This is Filbert." He pointed to the dog now sitting at his feet.

The pup looked her way and wagged as though approving of her presence.

"Do you have time for a chat?" Mr. Doss asked. The man reminded her of the sweet older friends of her grandmother.

"I guess so."

"Wonderful." He directed her to a concrete bench under an old oak tree in his front yard. The man smelled of spring soap and sunshine. The dog settled at his feet. "My wife and I placed this bench here in 1964. It's one of my favorite places to sit and enjoy God's nature."

She sat next to him, enjoying the soft breeze. "You sound like my Abuela."

"Your grandmother? Does she live in the area?"

Marie stuffed down the familiar longing rising within her. "No, she passed away a few years ago."

"I am very sorry for your loss. It's hard to lose those we love. My wife moved to heaven two years ago." His gaze seemed far off, filled with old private memories. "We raised six children in this house."

Marie stared into the distance. She couldn't imagine six

kids. She'd never had siblings, never had to worry about sharing a bathroom with anyone else, and never had the opportunity to have brothers and sisters to play with, talk to, or enjoy life together. "Do your children live in the area?"

"A daughter and her family live here in town. The others are scattered in Chicago, Idaho, Texas, and Alabama. I wish they all lived closer, but they have their own lives and families." Mr. Doss turned to her. "How about you? Where are you from? Where is your family."

Marie hesitated before deciding that giving a little information would be okay. "I grew up on the West Coast in a big city. No family anymore."

He patted her hand and squeezed before placing his hands back in his lap. "I'm sorry." The gesture didn't seem odd, just comforting. "I grew up here. I did travel a bit when I was in the Air Force. But basically, this town has been home for all of my eighty-one years. It's a good place to be. I hope you're happy here, Marie."

"Thanks. Me too." Even though her surroundings weren't safe where she grew up, at least she'd felt at home with her grandmother. If only she were here now.

They sat in silence for a moment. The only sounds were the quiet rustling of leaves in the breeze and a lawnmower in the distance.

Mr. Doss turned his gaze toward her. "Sometimes we try to recreate what we had so hard that we miss the new things God is doing. So, I'll pray you see the new things."

Unsure what to say, Marie nodded.

Mr. Doss pointed to a little bird chirping in the branches

above. "Do you notice the bird? The color of his wings, the stout little beak, the bright assessing eyes, the fragile legs as thin as the straw of a broom, the feet made for grasping a limb or twig. I'm not sure birds smile, but they sing. Do you sing, Marie?"

"I'm not much of a singer."

"As long as you have a voice, you can sing. Did you know God made your voice, so he loves to hear your voice?" He smiled as he looked her way. "You have a charming speaking voice. I'm sure your singing voice would be as pleasant." He paused for a moment. "Please forgive me. My wife used to teach piano and voice lessons, and she trained my ears to listen. But, of course, as I've gotten older, that's a little more difficult. But I am thankful I can hear the birds singing. There is always something to be grateful for. Do you have a favorite song?"

Marie shrugged. "I like all kinds, a mix of songs."

"Good for you. Some people limit their music and miss the beauty of variety." His gaze drifted off again before turning his deep blue eyes toward her. "You know we only see a small part of reality, like in a dim glass. We don't know all that is truly happening around us. There's more to the story. Much more."

She blinked, curious as to what he meant. There were things that could and couldn't be seen? Maybe like her life, visible yet hidden. What would it be like to see all of her reality, her entire life story?

Suspense novels kept her guessing until the end, but that wasn't as fun in real life. The Bible, Abuela, and even her driver had said all things work out for good for those who love God and are called according to his purpose. Unfortunately, Marie couldn't say she'd been very loving to God over the last few years. She'd barely prayed since her grandmother had passed away and hadn't been in church but one other time since then. Maybe it was time to make some changes.

A squirrel chattered as he ran along a branch in the magnolia tree, his movement dislodging two leaves that fluttered to the ground.

Growling, Filbert ran under where the furry critter taunted the little dog.

"Filbert, be nice." Mr. Doss stood. "The squirrel has as much right to the yard as you do."

The dog looked his way, huffed, and sat down, keeping his gaze on the intruder.

"Well, I better clean up that mess. I don't want the leaves blowing into the neighbor's yards. Of course, I doubt they would mind, but still, I'd like to do all I can to keep it clean."

"Can I help?" She rose to her feet.

"Thank you, but I think I can handle this. You probably want to get on with your walk. Thank you for stopping by and chatting. Please feel free to come by anytime. I enjoyed talking with you."

"Thank you, Mr. Doss. I enjoyed visiting with you too."

"One more thing." His smile gentle as he gazed at her. "Every day is a divine invitation to experience and discover more of God and what He has planned. Enjoy your day, Marie."

She grinned with a nod. *A divine invitation?* What if God

really did care for her and was inviting her to experience a new life and discover more of who he was?

Continuing her walk, she strolled around the neighborhood streets. Birds chirped and sang in the trees. Two birds, a robin, and a sandpiper, hopped in a yard as she passed by. She chuckled, wondering if Mr. Doss would describe the robin as wearing a gray suit with a red vest and the little stick-legged sandpiper as wearing a black scarf around the neck of his white body.

She'd been so paranoid watching people, worrying what might happen next. How much of the beauty around her had she missed?

Even though many of the houses were old, the yards were well-maintained, and most had flowers in planting beds or on the porches. Spring was fully embraced in Crawdad Beach, and the town seemed to have pride in keeping things neat.

Marie paused in front of a Tudor-style home with beautiful landscaping filled with blooming trees and flowers like those seen in the best gardening magazines. Her grandmother would have squealed with delight at this one. They couldn't afford many luxuries, but her grandmother used seeds or plant cuttings to produce a beautiful garden and abundant flowers in their tiny yard.

Marie checked the time. She needed to return to her place and prepare for her lunch date with David. She took one more look at the beautiful yard. In the old neighborhood, Abuela had made the best with what she'd been given; maybe it was time for her to do the same.

Chapter 7

Tantalizing smells enticed Marie forward as she stepped inside Tiddlywinks restaurant. A sign directed patrons to seat themselves. She sidestepped a waitress taking the order of the nice-looking middle-aged, dark-skinned gentleman who looked like the man she'd seen when she first drove into town.

Marie hurried to sit in the back before most people would notice her.

Since David wasn't scheduled to arrive for another ten minutes, she studied the menu, graced with a little cartoon crawdad wearing a chef's hat.

A curly-haired brunette with big brown eyes, holding a small pad and pen, stopped beside her table and smiled. "Hi, I'm Jennifer. What can I get you to drink?"

"I'm waiting for someone, but I'd love a glass of water. Thank you."

Jennifer nodded and rushed away.

Two businessmen walked past Marie's table. One stopped and looked at the other, "Brad's wife isn't much of a trophy wife. She's more of a trophy you'd get for just participating." The other man chuckled as they continued walking.

Ouch. Marie stared at a stain on her table. She'd never be considered a trophy wife, probably not even a participation trophy wife. She was more of a castoff.

To her right, two young women discussed the fun and challenges of raising children.

"I was able to take a nap yesterday." A cute blonde smiled as she sat straight in her chair.

"Really?" A weary brunette glanced at her friend. "How did you do it?"

"I laid beside her crib and was out like a light."

"I always feel guilty if I don't get things done. It's a constant battle just to keep the house semi-neat with the kids always in motion."

"I understand," the blonde said. "But my mom said to try and enjoy this phase of life even when it's hard. So maybe next time we get the kids together for a play date, we can help each other with house cleaning. I don't know why, but it's always easier to clean someone else's mess than mine."

The brunette recoiled. "That would be embarrassing."

"Oh, please." The blonde held up her fork, waving it toward her friend. "We all have messy lives and messy kids. We could make it fun."

The brunette sat still for a moment. "Okay, I'm in. It's worth a try."

Marie turned away. Would she ever have friends like that? Someone willing to be part of her messy life?

She turned her attention to the table to her left. Two older ladies chatted about trying to get their husbands to eat healthier. At another table, a group of women discussed a book they'd just finished reading.

Marie leaned closer to listen. She'd love to have friends to discuss the characters and storylines of the books she read.

A woman with salt-and-pepper hair tapped the cover of a book on the table. "This was my favorite book by this author. It was great."

An older women huffed. "Well, I think it had far too much kissing."

"Seriously?" A young, attractive, dark-skinned woman shook her head. "There were only a few scenes where the main character even kissed her boyfriend. It was great how they wanted to be together, but the author never went over the line."

"Yvonne thinks kissing is porno," The salt-and-pepper lady pointed to the older woman. "We're still unsure how she ended up with four children."

The rude lady crossed her arms over her ample chest. "That's different. We were married. I don't need to read that kind of stuff."

"So, you never kissed your husband before you married?" Salt-and-pepper lady asked. "You can keep your head in the sand, but I like reading stories about real people with real problems and how God redeems and restores lives."

A rousing refrain of affirmation went from the other ladies at the table.

The restaurant door opened, and David stepped inside. His gaze traveled around the room. When he noticed Marie, he beamed with a smile and walked towards her table.

"Sorry, I'm late. I had to take care of a few things at the store." He settled in the chair across from her. "Have you had a chance to look at the menu? Today's special is fried chicken breast. It's delicious and moist."

"Probably yummy, huh?"

A red tint crawled up his neck as he grinned. "Definitely yummy. They also have great fried okra and fried tomatoes. But, of course, if you get all that together, you wind up with a brown plate."

"Brown plate?"

"Yeah, you know everything on the plate is battered, friend, and golden brown." He rubbed his chin for a moment. "Then again, fresh vegetables would be better, huh?"

"Hi, David." The waitress stood beside their table. "What can I get y'all to eat?"

"Hi, Jennifer. This is Marie. She just moved here."

"I knew I hadn't seen you around." The waitress grinned. "Welcome to Crawdad Beach. It's nice to see another young person around here."

After they placed their order, David turned his attention to Marie. "So, what brings you to our little town?"

Marie shrugged. "I needed a change of scenery."

"Where did you move from?"

"New Mexico." At least, that was her last place of residence. "How about you? Have you lived here long?"

"Most of my life. I went away to college, traveled around Europe, and then worked in Chicago for a little while before I moved back. I missed family, the town, the people, and the area. It's a great place to live."

She couldn't imagine having a hometown she missed. When Abuela passed away, her life insurance money helped

Marie get out of the old neighborhood and into a decent apartment. She'd finished community college, found a great job, and even had her photo in the paper when she was promoted. But then, she had to leave almost everything behind as she went into hiding.

A short, round woman with silver hair and plump cheeks carried the food tray and set their order on the table. "David, who's your friend?"

"Mrs. Hollis, this is Marie. She just moved to our area."

"Well, it's nice to meet you." The lady smiled her way, a warm glow of welcome in her eyes. "Welcome to Crawdad Beach. Since you're new here, let us pick up your tab."

"That's very sweet but not necessary," Marie said.

"It's our pleasure. Enjoy your lunch with David. He's one of our favorites." Mrs. Hollis winked at him, then returned to the front counter.

"If you ever have any problems, see her." David motioned toward the woman. "She and her husband live above their restaurant. The rumor is she has a hotline to God."

"I think my Abuela had one too." Every day, her grandmother prayed out loud and sang praise songs, sometimes in English, sometimes in Spanish. The memory soothed and now frustrated her. Why hadn't she done the same?

"Is your grandmother still in New Mexico?"

"No, she passed away a few years ago."

"I'm sorry. I lost my grandmother too. I still miss her." David looked away momentarily, then reached for the saltshaker, his arm covered in scratches.

"What happened? Cat attack?".

David leaned forward, his gaze serious. "Rosebush. They might be pretty, but those things are deadly. Sure, they are given daily to people worldwide, but no one considers the thorns. The *deadly* thorns." He shuddered, then a slow grin crossed his face. "I was trimming the dead branches for one of my neighbors who's in her eighties. She's on blood thinners, so even a scratch could cause problems."

"That's kind of you." She'd never known anyone her age like David, with his cute sense of humor, and he even seemed kind and helpful. Marie turned her attention to the food and savored the moist fried chicken breast, green beans, and corn. Even the rolls were hot, fresh, and tasted homemade.

Would someone like David ever be interested in someone like her? Could she even dream of having any kind of relationship? Her life was one big question mark. She didn't know what tomorrow would hold and if she could stay here long-term. Maybe if they found the killer, she could be free.

David caught her staring and raised a brow in question. Heat crawling up her cheeks, Marie pointed to the menu with the crawdad wearing a chef hat. "I've heard of crawdad boils. Never had one, but I wonder how this little guy would think of something like that."

"Well, since he's our town mascot, we don't do crawdad boils. I think it would freak out the kids." David's expression was one of mock horror. "I can just imagine the rallies around town to save the crawfish." He chuckled, then composed himself. "What do you like to do with your spare time?"

Hiding from a killer probably wasn't what he wanted to

hear. "I enjoy being outside, walking at the beach, or reading books."

"Good choices. What kind of books do you like to read?"

"Suspense."

David nodded. "Another excellent choice. With a hero or heroine?"

"Heroine. Smart, tough, with a sense of humor. Dramatic without drama."

"Nice." David took a bite and chewed, then tilted his head as though contemplating. "Does your heroine ever need anyone's help?"

Interesting question. "At times. She can take care of herself but isn't afraid to ask for help. So, what do you like to do with your spare time?"

"Work on remodeling my house, going to the lake or beach, and I like to watch mystery movies."

"You like a mystery?"

He nodded and grinned. "I like trying to figure out things, who did what and why. Nothing gory, more like some of the old Sherlock Holmes stories."

"Good choice." Marie nibbled on a bite of chicken. If only true-life mysteries came with a quick solution. "You mentioned working on your house. I used to help my grandmother since something always needed fixing at her place." She'd taken on more projects than she could count since calling the creepy, smarmy, evil landlord was the last person they wanted in their house.

"A fixer woman." A look of admiration rested in David's gaze. "Can I hire you?"

She couldn't help but grin. David was definitely *not* creepy. "Perhaps."

"Great. That's settled, then. I'd love to show you around my house." He paused and held up his hands. "Don't worry. I could even have my sister and her kids with us when you come over. Maybe even my granddad. I'm sure he'd like to meet you."

"I think I'd like that." She could use a friend. Maybe his grandad would be like Mr. Doss. Marie glanced over David's shoulder at the front windows. Gray clouds had replaced sunshine. "Looks like a storm may be coming."

He followed her gaze. "We get pop-up showers on and off. Hopefully, it won't last too long."

"Who is this?" A shrill voice came from behind her.

Marie turned to see the sour woman who had been at the book club table.

David's jaw clenched as he shifted in his chair. "Mrs. Cowman, this is Marie." His voice wasn't rude but not too friendly.

The woman's steely gaze shot toward Marie, then turned back to David. "Well," she huffed. "Now I know why you're too busy to call my daughter." Turning her back, she marched out of the restaurant.

David took a deep breath and blew it out. "Sorry about that. I am *not* dating her daughter and will *never* date her daughter. Please don't take how she acts personally. Mrs. Cowman doesn't approve of anyone but herself. I would say she'll warm up to you, but she's probably never got above frigid with anyone." He shuddered and stabbed at his food.

Marie took another bite of her lunch, trying to erase the sour taste left by Mrs. Cowman. They needed a change of subject. "I have a question. When I first drove into town, I saw a woman on the street riding a lawnmower. Care to help me with an explanation."

David chuckled. "That's Lucy Guthrie. She moved here a few years ago from Idaho to live with her son. Believe it or not, she was in a lawnmower racer team known as Lawn-racing Lucy. I've seen the photos. Their mowers had racing engines in them. Can you imagine?"

Marie shook her head. "I had no idea."

"Crazy, huh? Because of a touch of dementia, she no longer drives her car. Fortunately, her son removed the blades and adjusted the engine to go at a low speed on her trusty mower. She lives on the next street from you in the bungalow on the corner."

Marie grinned as she continued to eat. Besides the episode with Mrs. Cowman, she was thoroughly enjoying herself. It had been too long since she'd felt comfortable with anyone, especially a man.

"My family has a cottage at the lake," David said. "It's a great place to get away for a day trip. We have jet skis. Have you ever tried that?"

"No, but it sounds fun."

"It's a blast, like riding a motorcycle on the water. So maybe we could do that one day if you want to try."

"That would be nice." She'd always wanted to try jet skiing, ride on the water, and let the wind whip through her hair.

Crash!

Marie's vision blackened at the sound, taking her back to that terrible day as the memory of gunshots echoed in her brain. Her breath closing off, she grabbed the table's edge to keep from throwing herself on the floor.

"Marie?" David's quiet, gentle voice came from far away. "Are you okay? That was just Jennifer dropping a plate." He touched her fingers.

She jolted away and forced her hands to rest on the napkin in her lap. Taking a ragged breath, she tried to focus on David's face and bring herself back to the present. She had to get a grip.

Trying to steady her breathing, she picked up her fork and moved the green beans around her plate. Why couldn't she have one day, one stinking day, when she could just enjoy herself?

"Have you noticed the murals around town with our Crawdad mascot?" David's voice was kind and gentle.

She blinked a few times, trying to clear her thoughts. Was David trying to get her mind off of what happened? She nodded.

"My sister painted the murals. She's a good artist. Do you paint?"

It took a moment for Marie to find her voice. "I can paint a wall."

He gave her a reassuring smile. "I know what you mean. I'm improving at painting walls."

She tried to focus, but her heartbeat continued to race, and her appetite was gone. "David, this has been nice. But I probably should get back to my place. I've got a headache."

He rose to his feet as she stood. "Thanks for meeting me. Maybe we can do something again sometime?" His voice was hopeful.

She turned to go, then stopped and faced him. "I'd like that."

Without another word, she hurried out of the restaurant. Why couldn't her life be different? Why couldn't she leave the past behind? She drove through the rain and continued driving.

Chapter 8

Waves scrapped the shoreline as black, angry clouds boiled on the horizon. Marie walked on the moist sand. She was finally having a nice time with a nice guy. Why did she have to react like that in the restaurant? It was only a dropped plate. But still, the sound had unlocked the vault where she kept the memory of that horrible day.

Why did sounds, smells, and senses trigger memories? Why couldn't she have a normal conversation, eat a regular meal, and act like an ordinary person?

She kicked the sand. David probably thought she was weird. The heroine in the novel she was reading would shake it off and move on with grace and humor. But being brave, strong, and resilient was easier said than done in real life.

This morning, everything had seemed right with the world, and now? Rain drizzled down, weeping tears from the sky. She stood there, just letting it soak her through and through. It didn't matter anyway. Her past continued to pursue her. She'd never be free, she'd always be on the run, never find a home where she could relax and enjoy life.

How could she ever forget that someone wanted her dead?

A truck with speakers blaring a screeching hard rock song drove slowly on the road.

She trembled and hurried back to her car, locked the door. If something happened to her, no one would know. There was no one to call, no one who would come to her rescue. All her family was dead, and she didn't know where Mr. Smith lived. Why couldn't she have died with her parents in the car wreck? Why did God abandon her?

Her car's windshield wipers tried to slap the rain away as she drove back to her place. Maybe she would just keep going. But where would she go?

She pounded on the steering wheel. *It isn't fair.* Nothing that happened was fair.

Hitting a patch of water on the road, the car hydroplaned and slid. Marie struggled to regain control. She had to get control not just of the vehicle but of her life.

Cranking up the radio, she searched for a song to match her mood. A female voice sang about being rescued. Oh, how she needed rescue.

David closed the store for the night as he mentally kicked himself for the thousandth time. Why hadn't he gone after Marie? He should have followed her out of the restaurant to make sure she was safe. But, instead, he just watched her go.

The sound of the dropping plate must have triggered a bad memory. Something had scared her in the past, but what? Is that why she'd moved to Crawdad Beach?

Maybe she was running from an abusive ex? The thought churned his stomach.

He would have called her to check, but he didn't have her number. Following her home probably would have freaked her out since she didn't like people to know where she lived. So, what was he supposed to do? He needed advice.

On autopilot, David drove through the rain to the home he'd visited since birth. He honked in greeting as a familiar car went the other way.

Stepping inside, he went to the family room where his favorite person in the world, with his dog in his lap, sat watching an old television show. "Hey, Granddad."

"Join me, David." He turned off the TV and turned to face him. "How's your day been?"

"Pretty good." David sat on the couch next to the old recliner. "I saw Aunt Helen's car. Did she come to visit?" His grandad's sister kept a close eye on him.

"Yes, she came by to drop off a casserole. Are you hungry?"

"No, I'm good. Thanks." David hadn't been able to eat a bite since lunch. He leaned forward. "I need advice."

His granddad's kind eyes met his gaze. "I'll help any way I can."

"I met someone for lunch today. She's new to the area and seems really nice. And she's cute. Okay, she's gorgeous. We met at Tiddlywinks, then Jennifer dropped a plate, and I could tell the sound scared Marie."

"Marie?" His granddad's head tilted as though contemplating. "Is that the girl's name?"

"Yes, Marie Delgado. She just moved here."

"Ah, I see. So, where did you meet Marie?"

"She came into the grocery store the other day, and we talked. I think you'd like her."

"I'm sure I would."

"After the plate thing, she left," David continued. "I wasn't sure what to do, so I just watched her go. I feel bad, but I didn't know what to do." He stood and paced in the small den. "I don't have her number, but I know where she lives. She's in the Bowman's duplex."

"Well, then Marie is living in a good place with good people. So, what advice do you need?"

"Should I swing by to check on her? Or maybe send flowers?"

His grandfather surveyed him. "Have you prayed and asked God for his advice?"

Heat crawled up David's neck. "No, sir."

"I think that's the best way to find out what to do, if anything, at this point."

"Marie seemed scared. I'm afraid something bad happened to her before. Even when she grinned, she remained guarded and a little sad."

"I'm sorry to hear that." A worried crease ran along his grandfather's face. "However, if you come on too strong, that might also scare her."

"Yeah, I think I'm having the knight saving the damsel in distress syndrome."

"You remember how those turned out." His granddad's gaze held no condemnation, only a reminder.

David stared at the floor. His track record with women wasn't too good. He tended to rush into relationships, wanting to fix everything for them. Plus, how he acted overseas had been far from godly.

His Grandad surveyed him. "Trust God for his forgiveness and move forward. As for Marie, let God lead in his timing and his way."

"But I want to help and make sure she's all right and feels welcome here. Maybe I could deliver her a welcome to Crawdad Beach gift bag from the grocery store."

"Does the store give welcome gifts?" One of Granddad's eyebrows raised.

"Not usually, but maybe we should start." David grinned. "I wish God would write out what I should do, make it plain and simple for my simple mind to comprehend because when I'm around Marie, my brain seems to take a vacation."

His granddad chuckled. "I understand. I was like that with your grandmother."

"Really? You?" David couldn't imagine his grandad as anything but well-spoken.

"She was a beauty. I was tongue-tied for a week before I could speak coherently. God blessed me with such a good woman. Much more than I deserved."

"Hey, you're a great guy. I'd like to have a marriage someday like that too."

"I pray you do, David. Remember to trust in the Lord with all your heart and not lean on your own understanding but in all your ways acknowledge God, and He will make your paths straight."

"Those verses are easier said than done. I'm trying, I really am."

"I know you are. God knows that too. Don't be so hard on yourself. We miss much of what God has for us because we don't trust him enough to enjoy what he has given us."

"Uh, I think I get what you're saying. Maybe."

"Trust God. Love God. And trust that God is loving and has your best interest at heart. And God also loves Marie and wants the best for her."

David stood. "Well, then maybe a welcome basket would be a good thing. I'll put something together and run by her place tomorrow."

His Grandad smiled. "It's a sweet thought and will be a sweet gesture." He opened his wallet and handed David a twenty. "I'll donate to the cause and pray for you both."

Chapter 9

How was she supposed to live while trying to shut down emotions as memories stayed with her?

Marie walked along the beach in the early morning rain-washed air. Last night, she'd tried to sleep but mainly tossed and turned, worried about what David probably thought about her. It wasn't like she could tell anyone what had happened and what might happen.

What if the killer was never caught? Would she always and forever be looking over her shoulder? How was she supposed to make a new life when she had no idea how long she'd be in this town or anywhere?

Marie sat down on the towel she'd brought with her. A man and woman jogged past. A squeal of laughter drifted on the breeze as a little boy played with a dog in the shallow surf while a couple watched from the shoreline.

Further down the beach, an older couple walked hand-in-hand, talking quietly as they strolled together. What would it be like to live with someone for years and love someone and be loved by them? Would it ever be possible for her? Besides Abuela, she'd always been the outcast, the loner.

The familiar ache of loneliness surging through her chest, Marie stood and let her feet carry her forward. The endless expanse of the ocean stretched before her.

Maybe she should just walk in and keep walking. Let the water engulf her, wash away all traces of her life. Would drowning be painful, or would she just drift away? No one would miss her.

A seagull screeched overhead. The waves churned, dragging the sand, the surf pounding and pounding louder and louder. The water crashed around her feet, pulling the sand from under her.

"Marie?"

Startled, she turned and looked into the kind, radiant blue eyes of Mr. Doss. His little dog, Filbert, stood behind his master.

"May we join you?" Without waiting for her reply, he guided her back to where she'd left her towel, then sat a folding chair next to her and settled in his seat. "After our rainy day, I thought a beach visit was appropriate. I hope we're not intruding on your time."

She swallowed hard and blinked away the moisture from her eyes as she sat on her towel. "No, it's okay."

"We come here often. It's peaceful by the ocean." Mr. Doss patted his dog. "Filbert, you may explore, but don't go too far."

The pup gave an approving wag, then trotted off to where the water reached the shoreline.

"He loves to look for crabs," Mr. Doss said. "Mind you, he enjoys looking for them but quickly learned not to bother them. Thus, the limp."

Marie pulled her knees up and wrapped her arms around them. Was she destined to always limp through life?

"Filbert's a rescue," Mr. Doss said. "Best we can tell, he's a lovely mix of Shi-Tzu, Bichon, and a touch of something else. He's been a blessing to the family. We all need rescue at one time or another."

She knew that feeling.

Filbert returned to his owner and sat at his feet. Two seagulls scurried along the waterline. The pup let out a low growl but didn't move as he watched the birds.

Mr. Doss patted his companion's furry head. "Filbert is well-behaved and seems to have come with his own training. Someone dropped him off a few years ago. We adopted him, and he adopted us. It's been good, I believe, for us all." He paused for a moment, then his tender eyes surveyed her. "Did you know there's a verse in the Bible that says God puts the lonely in families? It's true, you know. God is a good God."

She didn't know how to respond to that. She had no family. If God put lonely people in families, why had he deserted her?

"I was adopted," Mr. Doss spoke softly. "A kind couple took me in when I was four. I never met my father. My mother told me she was going to the store but never returned."

"I'm so sorry." She'd never imagined someone as gentle and kind would have had such a terrible start to his life.

"A story with heartache and pain can still be written with hope." He stood to his feet and folded his chair. "Well, I better get home. Thank you for allowing me to interrupt your morning."

She stood next to him. "I'm glad you did." Reaching down, she patted Filbert on the head. The little dog wagged, and if a dog could smile, he looked to be smiling.

"May I give you my phone number?" At her nod, he handed her his information. "Please call if you need anything or just want to talk. Always remember that God sees you and loves you."

Marie tucked the paper in her pocket.

Mr. Doss took a step, stopped, and turned toward her. "Sunday at our church, we're having a guest speaker. I've heard him before and think what he shares would bless you. If you're interested, the service starts at 9:30." He walked away with Filbert close by his heels. The man sometimes seemed angelic, almost like he had an internal glow. She half-expected him to disappear.

She turned her attention to the ocean, the waves mild and gentle. The breeze swirled around her as salty air cleansed her lungs. Mr. Doss's words echoed in her mind - *A story with heartache and pain can still be written with hope.* Would that be possible for her?

A catamaran glided across the water, skimming the surface. What would it be like to sail through life? Was that the key? Skim along, stop worrying about the past, and be hopeful for the future? Maybe the hopeful part of her story hadn't yet been written.

Back in town, Marie turned into her driveway. Something was on her porch. Had Mr. Smith sent something else? She parked her car and came around to check.

Curious, Marie carried the big basket with a bright yellow bow inside her house and closed the door. Unwrapping the gift, she grinned at the chocolate, coffee, recipes, kitchen goodies, and a mug with the cartoon Crawdad logo.

The tag, signed by David Mitchell, identified it as a Welcome to Crawdad Beach Gift basket from Mitchell's Grocery Store. Did he bring her the basket because that was common practice for new people in town, or did he send it because of what happened at the restaurant?

Whatever the reason, the gifts made her smile. People here had embraced her and made her feel welcome, or at least most of them. Growing up, she'd spent most of her time trying to survive.

Marie reached for her phone and dialed David's number. When the call went to voice mail, she left him a message thanking the store and him. Maybe, just maybe, she'd found a friend.

Her phone signaled an incoming text from Mr. Smith. In the coming week, he'd set up a job for her at a small manufacturing firm in the industrial park not far from where she lived. Once again, the man had gone beyond the ordinary.

How did he find work for her without so much as an interview? Maybe it would be like with a temp agency, sending people to companies. She'd probably be a contract employee with a temporary position leading to a possible permanent one.

But how did Mr. Smith make things happen, and why? Her grandmother would say she was blessed. Whether it was luck, blessings, or just how Mr. Smith worked, Marie was grateful for his help.

She put away the items from the basket and ate a quick lunch. Maybe the library had the next book in the series she was reading. Through a novel, she could pretend to be a brave, strong, daring heroine.

A few minutes later, she stepped inside the building and breathed deep the scent of a thousand stories. Surprised in a small town to find such a large selection, she ran her hand along the spine of the books in the mystery and suspense section as she searched for her favorite author. *Yes!* They even had the latest in the book series.

"May I help you?" The lady she'd seen at the grocery store with a white bouffant hairdo walked toward her.

"Yes, I'd like to check out this book."

"You must be the young woman who moved in at the Bowman place. Welcome to Crawdad Beach. I'm Maybelline Taylor. My husband and I are your back-door neighbors."

"Nice to meet you. I'm Marie Delgado. " As strange as it felt that most people knew where she lived and was new in town, it was time to embrace her life here.

"So, what brings you to our fair city?"

Marie momentarily studied the old wooden floor before meeting the woman's curious gaze. "A new story."

"Ha. Well put." The lady's brown eyes sparkled. "Between our little town and the book you've chosen, you've come to the right place. Let me put your information into our system and get you a library card."

Marie followed her to the office, which looked like the original train depot ticket counter.

Mrs. Taylor handed her a form to fill out and shared the hours they were open and the policies for the length of time a book could be kept. "Let me know if you want us to order another book. And, if you ever need recommendations, our book club actively reviews the latest and greatest novels."

"Thank you, that sounds great."

The door dinged as someone entered the library, and Mrs. Taylor hurried over to greet them.

Grateful for the distraction, Marie retrieved her driver's license to complete the information.

"Marie," Mrs. Taylor said. "I'd like to introduce you to Natalie Weaver." She pointed to a young woman holding a toddler.

"Hi." Natalie grinned as she tilted her head. "I remember you. You were having lunch with David Mitchell. He's such a nice guy."

"Yes on both counts." Marie recognized Natalie as the weary brunette lunching with her blonde friend at Tiddlywinks. She looked much better rested today.

"Marie just moved to our town," Mrs. Taylor said.

Natalie smiled. "My husband and I came to the area three years ago. I hope you like it as much as we do. " She turned her attention to the librarian. "Mrs. Taylor, do you have that new children's book I ordered?"

"Sure do. It's in the kid's section." She patted Marie's arm. "I'll be back in a few."

The ladies walked off, chatting about whatever book Natalie had ordered.

Marie leaned against the counter as she filled out the form. How interesting to meet people and have seen them before. Small-town living did have advantages.

"Sorry about that." The librarian stepped behind her

counter. "Let me get that library card for you." She entered Marie's information into the system, printed off a little card, ran it through a laminator, and handed it to her. "It's always good to have another reader in town. And since you like that author, I have other suspense authors I could suggest for you. We have an excellent collection of Christian fiction."

"Really?" Marie wasn't sure what to think about that genre.

"If you have time, I'd love to point out a few for you."

She followed the librarian as she explained which authors were her favorites.

Mrs. Taylor chuckled as she pointed to one. "When I read her books, it's like the author grabs you by the throat and won't let you go until the last page. It's great suspense without gore." She pointed to another author. "This one writes with mystery and a touch of romance. Nothing too graphic." She pointed to another group. "These have a comedy with their suspenseful stories. And this one has a touch of the supernatural. They write from a Christian worldview. They're Christians, and that gently spills into their stories."

The librarian pointed to the book Marie had in her hands. "Since you like that author. May I suggest this one?" She handed her a paperback. "The author will keep you on the edge of your seat or reading up into the night. She's a master of suspense, and her heroine is smart and fun."

Not wanting to disappoint the kind woman, Marie accepted the book. Maybe she could take it home and bring it back when she returned. "Okay. I'll give it a try."

"Oh, goodie." Mrs. Taylor hurried to the checkout

counter. "You won't be disappointed. I look forward to hearing what you think."

Marie thanked her, returned to her place, and plopped on the couch. Maybe she'd spend a few minutes reading the author the librarian suggested.

Rubbing her eyes, she glanced at the clock. How had she read for six hours straight? Lost in the great storyline, she'd even missed eating supper.

Heading to the kitchen, Marie snagged a handful of almonds and then went to look out her front window.

A group of people stood talking in front of Mr. Doss's house. Laughing and squealing, little children ran around the giant oak tree with Filbert chasing them.

Marie's vision blurred with longing. Turning away, she went back to the novel, back to an imaginary world where, in the end, everything would turn out okay.

Chapter 10

Waiting until ten in the morning had been agonizing. Time couldn't go fast enough. Marie's sandals slapped against the sidewalk as she hurried to the library. She'd stayed up most of the night finishing the novel the librarian had recommended.

Marie had to get the next one in the series. The heroine in the story had plenty of problems, yet the author created a beautiful, hope-filled, soul-satisfying story. It was almost like the writer knew Marie's struggles and had given her something that brought her closer to God. How could a fictional story even do that?

She smiled at the mural of the cartoon crawdad and stepped inside the building. "Good morning." Marie greeted the librarian as she made her way to the fiction section.

"Hi, Marie. Did you enjoy the book?"

"Yes. I loved it. Thank you for the recommendation. Do you have more books by her?"

"Oh, yes. She's written for years, and I've loved everything I've read." Mrs. Taylor picked one of the author's books off the shelf and handed it to Marie. "This one is the next in her series. It made me laugh, cry, and kept me up late into the night. It's an exciting page-turner."

"The last one you gave me did too. I wish I had known

about the author sooner. It was great to read something that entertained me and gave me things to think about. Good things, you know?"

"Yes," Mrs. Taylor nodded. "And I tell you, her characters are so real. One day, I found myself at the clothing store thinking about how cute the heroine would look in an outfit. Thank goodness I didn't buy it."

Marie chuckled as she followed the librarian to her office. "I'll admit I wish her heroine were my friend. I'd love to sit and talk with her."

"Wouldn't that be fun? A few years ago, one author had a website where her imaginary characters blogged. Writers can get pretty creative. Have you ever written anything?"

"No, I'm not much of a writer."

Mrs. Taylor leaned against the counter, a faraway look in her eyes. "I wish I could write. Make up exciting stories. Mysteries with sweet romances, but the main romance would be as the characters learned more about the divine romance."

"Divine romance?" Marie tilted her head. Even Mr. Doss said every day was a divine invitation.

"Yes, the romance with God. He made each of us, and His perfect love tenderly beckons us to come to His love. Just think of the possibilities." Mrs. Taylor sighed. "But at least as a librarian, I can point readers to those who write great stories." She tapped the book Marie had in her hands. "This one will be a blessing. I can't wait to hear what you think. I'm glad God brought you to us, Marie."

"I am too." It was nice to say that and mean every word. She was grateful she'd been brought to Crawdad Beach.

Before starting the book, she needed to stop by the store and put together a few lunch items since she'd be starting a job in a few days. The thought of starting work somewhere she'd never been, never even interviewed, and had no earthly idea what she would be doing made her want to run and hide.

Couldn't she stay in her nice little duplex and read or spend time at the beach? Then again, she did need to support herself in some way. Mr. Smith had been so kind to her. Abuela would say God had been kind to her. Right now, she'd agree.

David tried to rub his frigid fingers back to life after spending forty-five minutes stocking food in the freezer. Ten thirty in the morning, and besides his usual day of placing orders with vendors, checking products and deliveries, and working with the staff and customer service, he'd checked the budget, made sure prices were set correctly on the items, and ensured everything was running smoothly.

Plus, he'd cleaned up a broken pickle jar, rescued a toddler who had crawled behind the cereal boxes, and fixed the wobble in a grocery cart. The glamorous life of a store manager never ended.

David returned to his office and checked his phone. His dad had left a text saying they were arriving back in town late tonight. He was looking forward to seeing his parents, and hopefully, his dad would be back in the store to help.

At the sound of his name being called, he turned.

Brenda, one of the store's cashiers, stood in his office doorway. "Would it be okay if I took off later today?" Her big blue-eyed gaze looked hopeful. "I need to take... uh, my granny to the doctor."

David rubbed his neck, trying to think who might be able to cover her position, maybe Tony. "Sure, I'll figure something out."

She laid her warm hand on his arm. "I knew I could count on you."

He took a slight step back. Brenda was cute but only eighteen and far too friendly. Before working at the store, he'd decided never to date employees.

Brenda ignored his discomfort and stepped closer. "I'll come in as soon as I get her settled tomorrow afternoon, okay?" She fluttered her eyelashes.

"That's fine." David picked up a clipboard from his desk and held it in front of him—a barrier to keep her from getting closer. "I need to take care of a few things."

After Brenda left, he pushed open the stock room door and found his big friend stacking boxes. "Hey, Tony, I have a favor. Can you work Brenda's shift this afternoon at her register?"

"Be glad to help." Underneath Tony's bushy mustache, he knew there was a smile. "Remember, May Branch is delivering their produce tomorrow morning."

"That's right. I'll come in early and take care of everything." Even though it meant extra work, David enjoyed visiting with the owners of May Branch Farms. Steve and Paula were great people. That was one of the nice things about managing a small store. He got to know clients and many of the local farmers.

"I have a date tonight." Tony's voice was so quiet he could barely be heard.

David tried to stop his mouth from hanging open. "You do?" Tony might be a big, former college lineman, but he had no confidence around women. "Who's the lucky girl?"

"She's the daughter of a friend of my mom's friend. We've emailed a few times. She lives by the beach, so we're meeting at a restaurant and then going to a movie."

"Wow, this is a big thing for you. Way to go."

"What if she doesn't like me or I don't like her? What if I don't know what to say?" Everybody uses text, email, or social media. I don't know that I can talk in emojis."

David chuckled. "Well, those are the dangers of in-person dating. You'll be fine. I'm sure you'll survive. And if nothing else, it should be interesting."

His friend huffed out a breath. "I'll be glad when it's over."

"Think positive. No matter what happens, you'll have a good meal and see a good movie."

"Okay, I can do that." Tony turned and easily moved a stack of boxes that probably weighed several hundred pounds. With Tony in the building, they would never need a forklift.

When his friend returned to work, David stepped out of the back.

"Hi, David." Alexa zipped past. "I need to pick up a few items for our break room."

David chuckled as Alexa power-walked past him. Her days as a track star might have ended, but she never seemed to slow down. She talked fast and moved even faster.

Maybe it was time for him to move forward with Marie. Since tomorrow was Saturday, maybe she'd take him up on the jet ski offer.

David straightened a box of cereal about to fall off the shelf. Since there had been a run on that brand, he made a mental note to order additional next month.

"Hi."

He jumped at the soft voice. As he turned, his hand connected with the shelf. Boxes scattered across the floor.

"I'm so sorry." Marie hurried to help as he scooped up as many as he could. "I didn't mean to startle you."

Heat swarmed up his neck and settled on his face. "Sorry. I was thinking and didn't see you." He arranged the boxes back in their proper place.

"Thinking and looking is tough to do at the same time.

He loved the sound of her light and sweet laugh. "I have lousy peripheral vision. Sports injury. Fastball to the head." Maybe that's why he was barely coherent when Marie was around.

"Oh no, I'm even more sorry. I didn't mean to laugh."

"No, it's okay. I just didn't see you."

"Thank you again for the gift basket. That was very thoughtful."

"I'm glad you liked it." He stepped closer, watching the uncertainty in her gaze. "Are you doing okay?"

Her smile dipped, then partially rebounded. "Yes, I'm

sorry I ran out on you at the restaurant."

"It's okay. I should have followed you to make sure you were okay. I was wondering. We talked about maybe jet skiing sometime. Would you maybe like to go with me this Saturday? I mean, if you'd like to. If it'd be okay." David rubbed the back of his neck. He had to stop saying okay. No wonder he was still single.

Her gaze dropped to the floor for a moment. She took a deep breath and looked his way. "Yes, I would like that. That sounds fun."

"Great. Can I pick you up at your place, say seven in the morning? That's when the water's best, or is that too early? If it is, I can pick you up later if you want me to. I could even give you directions if you want to drive yourself. But I could pick you up. That would probably be easier. Would that be okay?" David clamped his mouth shut. He might as well crawl and hide behind the cereal boxes since he sounded like a blubbering idiot.

"Picking me up at seven would be fine. Do I need to bring a towel or anything?"

"Just bring something you don't mind getting wet and a change of clothes for later. We have towels at the lake house. I'll pick you up. If that's still okay."

"Okay," Marie drew the word out with a smile. "I'll see you Saturday morning."

David watched as she walked away. When she'd turned the corner, he pumped his fists in the air. *Yes!* He had a date with Marie.

Chapter 11

Water spraying her face and wind whipping in her hair, Marie laughed as she raced her jet ski beside David. He'd told her she would have fun, but she had no idea what a thrill it was to fly along the surface of a lake.

Laughing, he glanced her way. "Come on, slowpoke!" Passing Marie, he then slowed so she could come alongside. "Let's head to the other shore."

Cloud cover kept the sun from being too hot as they traveled across the vast lake. She'd never felt so free. Laughing, David raced ahead of her.

A ski boat zoomed between them, causing the water to swell with choppy waves. Marie struggled to maintain control as a big wave crashed against her craft. Throttling hard, she gave the jet ski more power. The watercraft zoomed out of the water and sent her flying.

Sputtering and flailing in the water, she tried to get her bearings. Thank goodness the thing had a kill switch and she'd worn a life vest.

David maneuvered next to her. "Are you okay? Can I help?"

"I'm fine. Just lost control." Embarrassed, she clung to the side of the jet ski.

"Put your hand on the handle and pull yourself up. You

may need to use your other hand to help stabilize as you climb back on."

Grunting, she did as David suggested. Thankfully, she had enough upper body strength she could get back on. So much for being ladylike as she wobbled back on her seat.

She tried to restart her engine, but the machine only gave a weak sputter. David made several suggestions, but the jet ski wouldn't start no matter what she tried.

"Hold tight. Let me see if I can try something else." He stood on his craft, popped open the seat, and then held up a rope for her to tie onto the handles. "I'll tow you behind me. Unfortunately, it could take a while. If we don't go slow, pressure can force water back through the exhaust system and flood the engine."

Just her luck, first date, and she broke their jet ski. "I'm sorry. I hope it can be fixed."

"Don't worry. I've had it happen to me, too. Hold on, and I'll get you back to the dock."

Clouds darkening, the wind picked up, making the water more and more choppy. Thunder rumbled in the distance. Marie shuddered at the sound and the cooler temperatures.

David held up his hand, signaling he was cutting off his engine, then waited as her jet ski floated closer to him. "I'm such a dunce. I forgot we installed a water shut-off valve after the last time this happened. I hate to ask you to do this, but could you jump off for a minute while I work on your engine?"

She dropped into the choppy water and watched as he went to work.

In only a few minutes, he finished. "Okay, I got

everything ready for towing so we can go faster." He jumped off her machine, then held it as still as he could while she got resettled. "I'm sorry I didn't remember this sooner."

Back on his watercraft, he increased his speed, pulling her behind him.

Fifteen minutes later, they were safe at his parent's covered dock.

Marie took his hand as he helped her off her jet ski. "I'm sorry again about what happened."

"Hey, you're a newbie, so don't worry. That's part of the fun." He raised both jet skis from the water using an electric boat lift. "It should be fine by this afternoon. Let me grab our dry clothes." David unlocked the door of the small room where they had earlier dropped off their belongings. He placed their life vests inside, next to fishing poles and other items used by his family. He grabbed two beach towels and handed one to her so she could dry off.

Towel swaddled around her; she stood beside him as they watched the rain.

David gave her an apologetic grin. "I had planned on a fun, trouble-free, sunny day."

"Don't worry, it's been a great day."

"I'm glad you came." David leaned toward her, his gaze resting on her lips.

Marie's heartbeat whooshed in her ears as he leaned toward her.

Two speedboats raced by on the lake, drawing his attention. He cleared his throat, straightened, and stepped back. "Looks like the rain has let up. Let's go to the cabin where we can change. I'll make us lunch."

David unlocked the door and led her inside. "What do you think? Mom had it redone last year."

The cabin's interior exposed logs were painted white. A floor-to-ceiling stone fireplace was flanked by French doors leading to the deck that ran along the back of the house. Modern light fixtures, leather furniture, white kitchen cabinets with wooden countertops, stainless steel appliances, and a large dining table with eight chairs completed the space. Although the room was decorated to the hilt, it still had an inviting, casual feel. "This is really nice."

"I know, right? Mom's a builder, so she couldn't wait to get in here and redecorate. She left the exterior in its rustic form but loved getting the inside updated." He pointed to the hallway. "You can change in the master bedroom on the left since it has a bathroom. I'll change in one of the other bedrooms."

Marie hesitated. She trusted David, but this was their first time alone. She waited until he left, then stepped inside the room and locked the door behind her. Large windows overlooked the lake. The room was decorated with a king-sized bed, a dresser, nightstands, and two light teal plush chairs that faced the outside view. She could imagine how sweet it would be to wake up and gaze at the water.

Paintings of the lake at sunset graced the walls, and several family photos sat on the dresser. Stepping closer, she studied a group photo of children of various ages. What looked to be the little boy version of David sat on the lap of an Asian woman who must have been his grandmother. The other kids, smiling and laughing, sat beside her.

After changing into a casual sundress and sandals, Marie entered the family room and gazed out the French doors. The deck overlooking the lake was a perfect spot for relaxing. She could picture herself reading a novel on one of the chairs.

"Nice view, huh?" David, dressed in shorts and a t-shirt, walked toward her.

"It is. Do you get to come here a lot?"

"Not as much as I used to since I bought my house. Working on renovations keeps me pretty busy. Would you like something to drink? We have water, sodas, and lemonade."

"Lemonade sounds great."

A few minutes later, David returned with the drinks. "I'll wipe off some of the chairs if you want to sit outside."

Marie followed him to the deck and waited while he dried off their seats. Large trees surrounded the property, filtering the sunshine. The storm had passed, leaving the sky a bright blue and the air washed clean.

David waited until she settled, then sat next to her. "My grandparents bought the cabin in the early '70s, and it's been a fun place for the family ever since."

"Must be nice." Marie couldn't imagine having a place like this with fun family memories. She didn't even know what it was like to have a family.

"You ought to come over in the evening. The sunset over the lake can be spectacular. I could meet you here after I get off work sometime."

"I'd like that." Marie leaned back in her chair. "I start a

new job Monday morning, so an evening by the lake would be nice."

"Where will you be working?" David asked.

"Lawson Manufacturing."

"That's a good company. The owners are great people. I've known them most of my life."

"That's nice to know." At least that sounded promising. Thank goodness he didn't ask her what she would do since she still had no clue.

"I hope you're enjoying living here." David's gaze studied her.

"I am. I wasn't sure what to expect, but Crawdad Beach has been as friendly as their welcome sign."

He grinned, stretched out his legs, and sighed in contentment.

Sitting in comfortable silence, they sipped their lemonade. A ski boat, pulling a wakeboarder, passed in the distance. A small sailboat drifted along the water. Children's laughter came from a nearby house.

"So," David grinned at her. "what did you do when you were a kid for fun?"

She stared at the water as she tried to think. Their neighborhood had been terrible. But still, she hadn't had a bad life with Abuela, just not what someone would think as fun. "I helped my grandmother take care of the house and garden."

David's friendly gaze continued to survey her. "When we ate lunch together, you said you liked to read. Did you read a lot when you were younger?"

"Yes, we'd go to the library so I could check out as many

books as they let me." Now that she thought about it, that was one of her more fun memories. She could escape into the stories, live anywhere in the world, and be anyone she wanted. She turned toward him. "Did you like to read when you were younger?"

He grinned and shrugged. "Not really. I like to read now, but back then, I was into outdoor activities and sports."

"Ah, the macho guy."

His face tinged pink as he chuckled. "I don't think I've ever been called that before."

She was surprised at his reaction. As handsome as he was, she'd have thought he'd have lots of girls and be sure of himself. "What was your favorite sport?"

"Baseball. I was pretty good. Even had a college scholarship to play until I broke my wrist." He grimaced as he rubbed his arm.

"I'm sorry. What position did you play?"

"Pitcher. Had a mean fastball, too. Did you ever play sports?"

Marie shook her head. "Not really. Mainly martial arts."

"Cool. Did you get one of those belts?"

"Yes, a black belt in Taekwondo."

"Wow, I'm impressed."

She chuckled and playfully narrowed her eyes. "Yeah, you better watch out."

"I'll be good." David held up his hands as though surrendering. "I can't imagine being a black belt. Some kids thought that since I had Asian blood, I'd automatically know karate and be good at math."

"People do categorize, don't they?" She'd been placed in all sorts of categories. Not many of them were what she wanted.

"I figure we're all human." David smiled and leaned toward her. "All of us made by God and descended from Adam and Eve. One race, the human race. You've mentioned your grandmother has passed, but what about the rest of your family, siblings, parents?"

She took a deep breath and tried not to think about what she would share. "No siblings. No other family. My parents died in a car wreck when I was a baby. Abuela had no remaining family and was a widow."

David's eyes rounded. "Oh, that's tough. I'm really sorry." His voice was quiet, subdued.

"Not your fault."

David squeezed her hand, his brown eyes filled with kindness. "Really, I am very sorry for all you've been through."

Marie lowered her watery gaze to where his hand rested on hers. She didn't want to cry, didn't want to embrace David's thoughtfulness, yet she did. She was tired of being tough, stuffing down her emotions, and being isolated and alone.

She rose to her feet and walked to the deck railing. The lake stretched before her, the water shimmering in the sunlight. If only she could drown her past, keep only the good memories, let go of the rest, and step into a new life. But the past remained with an uncertain future.

He came next to her. "You don't have any idea how

wonderful you are, do you?"

She drew in a deep breath and swiped a tear that escaped down her cheek.

David took her in his arms and held her close. His heartbeat steady and strong in his chest.

She sank into his embrace, longing to belong, to have a new life. Tears welled and ran down her cheeks.

Chapter 12

In the early morning light, Marie watered the flowers on her back porch. After her emotional outburst at the lake, David grilled burgers, and they sat on the deck and spent hours talking about music, movies, books, and various subjects.

Although they were still basically strangers, it felt like they had been friends for years. He even invited her to attend his church but didn't push.

The few guys she'd dated had always wanted more and tried to cross her boundaries. David was different. He'd driven her home and walked her to the front door. Not ready for the day to end, she had leaned into his kiss before he could change his mind, or she'd chicken out.

At the memory, she rubbed her fingers across her lips. David was kind, compassionate, and tender. With him, she felt safe, cherished. But would a guy like him want to continue dating her? What did she have to offer?

Marie sighed. She probably could pray and ask God, but since she'd not spoken to him very much, would he even listen? Maybe she could get some answers if she went to church. David invited her to the same one Mr. Doss attended, and they seemed to have their lives together.

Mr. Doss had said something about a guest speaker. Maybe today would be a good day to visit. She could sit in the back and check out things. And, if she saw David, that would be a bonus.

It took her forty-five minutes to decide what to wear before choosing a sundress and a light sweater to cover her bare shoulders. Taking a deep breath, she stepped into the church lobby. A young woman greeted and welcomed her, then directed her to a small coffee bar with free donuts.

Not at all what Marie expected. Abuela's church had been friendly, but only a few people attended each week. In another church Marie had visited once, most people had dressed in suits, and the women had their hair pulled back so tight their faces seemed puckered in displeasure.

Here, the people milling about all seemed normal. Some dressed well, while others wore casual attire. The people looked comfortable and happy. Even a group of teenagers joked and laughed.

Mr. Doss, with a brass-topped wooden cane that looked like something she would have imagined a gentleman using in old England, stood near the entrance to the sanctuary, chatting with another older man.

A smile lit his face when he spotted her, and he waved her over. "Marie, I'm glad you came. This is Chester Taylor. His house is right behind your place."

Marie recognized him as the man at the grocery store with the sugary cereal that had nuzzled his wife's neck.

Mr. Taylor shook her hand. "I heard a sweet young woman now lived in the Bowman place. It's nice to meet you. I think you know my wife, the librarian."

"Yes, she's very nice."

He smiled. "She's a keeper. If you ever need anything, just holler."

"Thank you. I appreciate the offer."

"Well, I better go and find Maybelline before the service starts. Henry, are we still on for fishing on Tuesday morning?"

"I'll be ready to go at five." After he left, Mr. Doss turned to her. "I'm glad you came."

"Thank you." She gave a curious glance as she pointed at his cane. "I didn't know you needed one. Are you okay?"

His grin took a mischievous turn. "I had my hip replaced, and my family thinks I need to always keep one with me. I only use it when they're around. And, maybe someday, I'll use it to bop a bad guy."

She coughed a laugh as he led her to a pew toward the back.

A small band with guitars, drums, a keyboard, and several singers led them in songs as the words displayed on a big screen at the front. She did a double take when she noticed David playing an acoustic guitar. The guy had even more hidden talents.

Some of the music she hadn't heard before, but others were familiar. Moisture built in her eyes as they sang one song about God's mercy and grace. She'd forgotten how much she'd enjoyed the time of worship.

After a brief introduction by the pastor, a tall, stocky man with slicked-back black hair and tattoos covering his arms and neck stepped onto the stage. The man told how he'd been left at thirteen to fend for himself and got involved in a life of crime, drugs, and things he was too ashamed even to mention.

He'd been arrested and sent to prison. While there, he'd been told about Jesus, the one who loved him regardless of the terrible things he'd done and that had been done to him. Spellbound, Marie watched and listened.

"Perhaps you know Jesus," the man said. "You know his name. Maybe you've even prayed to him. But, have you asked him to come into your heart and made him Lord of your life? Christianity isn't just a word, it's about a relationship with the one who loves you best. Your mother and father may desert you. Your friends and family may desert you, but God and his Son, Jesus Christ, will never leave or forsake you." And then, he looked right at her, "Ven a casa con Jesús, él te está esperando."

Marie stifled a gasp. Why would he tell her to come home to Jesus because he was waiting for her? Her heartbeat racing, Marie rubbed her forehead to hide her face. Did this man know who she was? Was she again in danger?

She checked Mr. Doss's reaction. Seemingly unconcerned, his gaze stayed on the speaker. She knew Jesus was supposed to love her, but where had he been all those years when everyone she loved died, and where was God when she had to run for her life?

The man on stage continued talking in English as he surveyed the crowd. "Jesus Christ gives you a new life. In Christ, you receive a new identity as a beloved child of the King of kings. No matter what has been done to you or what you have done, Jesus Christ waits with open arms. He is the only place your soul is eternally safe."

She'd love to be forever safe. But nothing could change

her past, and no one could guarantee her future.

"Come home to Jesus," the man said. "He holds your heart in His tender nail-scarred hands." Walking the stage, he invited people to come to the one who loved them. The man then closed with a passionate prayer.

The pastor joined him and invited anyone who wanted to come to Jesus to walk to the front, and someone would talk with them.

Music started playing, and even though part of her wanted to talk to someone, she held onto the pew in front of her. She wanted to trust Jesus with her life and give him her heart, but she'd grown up in church, and still, bad things happened.

The service ended, and Mr. Doss turned to her. "Thank you for coming. I hope it was a blessing. Would you like to come over for lunch? My family will be there, and we always have plenty to share."

Wanting time to think about what the man had said, she declined his offer.

He nodded, then placed his hand on her arm. "I'm always available if you need to talk."

Her vision blurred at his kindness. "Thank you." She hurried to her car before she ran back into the church.

Back home, Marie threw her purse on the couch and stepped out on her patio. Tears gathering and pooling in her eyes, she looked up at the ceiling. "Where were you, God? Why did you leave me?"

A song played from the Bowman's patio next door. Marie leaned against the wall, listening as a woman's voice sang about God's rescue. Marie's breath squeezed in her throat. Why hadn't she been rescued?

She sat in a chair as her thoughts took another direction. Her parents had died, but she'd been rescued. Her grandmother had died, but God had provided for Marie's next steps. God had rescued her from being shot by the man. God had rescued her by providing a hiding place in New Mexico and now in South Carolina. God rescued her by providing Mr. Smith to take care of her. Had she all along been rescued? Could it be true?

Marie ran to get her grandmother's Bible. What was that verse again about forgetting the past and God doing new things? She sat on the couch and ran her hand along the teal handmade cloth cover of the Bible. Was something inside?

As she lifted the cover, an envelope fluttered to the ground. *Para mi amada nieta.* For her beloved granddaughter. Her grandmother had written a letter to her.

Tears coursing down her cheeks, Marie curled up on the couch and slowly read the words as though hearing Abuela's sweet voice.

Dear one, God created you, weaving you together in your mother's womb, and He knows the plans He has for you, plans for a hope-filled future. God's love is unfailing and eternal. He will never leave or forsake you, and no one can snatch you out of His hands.

God's steadfast love and mercies never end; they are new every morning, and His faithfulness is so very great. Trust the

Lord with all your heart. Rely on Him, put Him first, and He will show you the way to go.

Be strong and let your heart take courage. Don't worry about anything; instead, pray about everything. Tell God your needs, and don't forget to thank Him for His answers, and God's peace will be with you. God's peace is far more wonderful than our human minds can understand and will keep your thoughts and your heart quiet and at rest as you trust in Jesus.

Even though there is trouble in the world, Christ has overcome the world, and He will be with you and give you His peace, so don't let your heart be troubled or afraid.

People can do terrible things, but God __will__ punish those who do wrong. Remember to trust in God, and don't be fearful of people. Be strong and brave, and don't be afraid or discouraged, for God is with you wherever you go.

When your heart is breaking, the Lord is near, and He will heal your broken heart and gently wrap your wounds in His tender love. When you need a friend, remember that Jesus called His followers His friends. He's a Father to the fatherless, even putting the lonely in families.

Don't keep looking back on the past, for God will do something new, making a way where there doesn't seem to be a way. God is a loving, rescuing, restoring Father. Remember, nothing is impossible with God.

Nothing can ever separate you from God's love -- not death, life, angels, demons, things in the past or future; no power, height, depth, or any other created thing will be able to separate you from God's unlimited love, which is in Christ

Jesus our Lord.

How I pray that your heart is open so that you will know God's hope-filled calling on your life. For you are God's workmanship, His own master work of art, created in Christ for good works, which God prepared for you before you were even born. So, whatever you do, put forth your very best effort as working for God and not just for people.

Always love the Lord your God with all your heart, soul, and mind. He loves you, dear one—delight in the Lord, and He will give you the desires of your heart.

One day, we will all be together. I love you forever and always.

Abuela

Chapter 13

I'm praying you have a great day at your new job.

Marie grinned at David's text. She'd slept longer, deeper, and better than in years. Last night, she'd poured out her heart to God and talked to him more than she had ever in her whole life. And then she'd spiritually taken her heart and handed it to Jesus, asking him to be the Lord of her life.

She'd never felt freer. Today truly was a new day with new beginnings.

Marie straightened her blouse and checked her slacks. When she'd driven by the company the other day to see what the employees wore, most were in jeans and casual outfits. However, a few people had dressed in business casual. She hoped she'd chosen a proper outfit since she'd be working in the main office.

She hurried to the kitchen and stared at the lunch she'd packed. Should she take it with her? Leave it in the car? Or, hope for the best that she'd have time to get lunch somewhere. What if she was too nervous to eat? She shoved it in the refrigerator and take her chances.

The drive didn't take long before she reached her destination. The surrounding businesses had minimal landscaping, but not Lawson Manufacturing. Large palm trees, bushes, and blooming crepe myrtles rimmed the company parking lot. The sweet scent of blooming flowers lining the sidewalk propelled her to the front door.

"Good morning, you must be Marie." A woman with shoulder-length salt-and-pepper hair smiled and stood. "I'm Trudi Lawson."

Marie returned the greeting and shook the lady's outstretched hand.

"We're glad you're here." Trudi led her to an office behind the reception area. "Mr. Lawson, my husband, has been expecting you."

"Brad, this is Marie." She addressed a big man with silver hair, his face relatively wrinkle-free.

He rose from behind a paper-strewn, massive oak desk and came around to greet her. "Welcome to Lawson Manufacturing. Have a seat." He pointed to the burgundy leather chairs in front of his desk. "Thank you, Trudi." He winked at his wife, then settled back at his desk.

Mr. Lawson surveyed her for a moment. "Your recruiter, Mr. Smith, told us so much about you. Fascinating man." He stared into space momentarily before his brown-eyed gaze settled back on her. "Your college transcript is very impressive. You must have worked hard."

Marie nodded. Thank goodness Mr. Smith transferred her transcript into her new name. "Yes, sir. Doing my best is important to me."

"That's good to hear. You'll be a great asset to our team. And we're grateful to have another bi-lingual employee. Our company may not be the biggest, but we provide residential and commercial customers with porcelain stone, glass, and natural stone tile."

"Your company has great ratings."

"Good. You checked us out."

"Yes, sir." Thank goodness she'd spent time on the Internet researching the company information.

"So, are you ready to get started?" At her nod, he stood and directed her to the door. "Let me show you around the facility." Mr. Lawson knocked and opened the door to the first office. "This is Nate, he's our operations manager. Nate, this is Marie. She's replacing the void left by Mrs. Box."

Smiling, the dark-skinned man, probably in his thirties, rose to his feet. "Welcome to the company."

They chatted for a few minutes, and then Mr. Lawson took her to the next office with two cubicles.

He stopped at the first one and introduced her to Grace, a young woman dressed in black slacks, a matching jacket, and a white pressed cotton shirt. Her brown hair was neatly pulled back in a ponytail. She stood, pushed her glasses on her nose with one hand, and clutched a folder against her chest with her other. "It's nice to meet you."

A head popped up from the next cubicle. A young woman with a lightning bolt shaved into short, dark hair waved. "Hey, I'm Alexa. Welcome to the company."

Mr. Lawson shook his head. "Alexa has the energy of a hyperactive hummingbird."

"I heard that." The young woman shot a playful glare at the big boss.

"Of course you did." He chuckled. "Alexa is our resident track star with super-sonic hearing."

Grinning, Alexa hurried toward Marie. "Grace and I are going to Tiddlywinks for lunch today. We'll get you on our way out. You'll love working here."

Marie grinned. She might be clueless about her job, but at least she didn't have to worry about lunch.

Mr. Lawson pointed to the office across the hall. "This is where Max works when he's in town. He's our salesman and is usually on the road. He should be in later today."

He stopped at the last door before entering the manufacturing area. "This will be your office."

She had her own office? Just what had Mr. Smith told them she could do? The room contained a desk, chair, file cabinets, a computer, and a credenza. A large window framed the pink-flowering crepe myrtles outside. The office looked beautiful and comfortable.

"Most of your work will be done here, but we will need you to fill in out front at times, and you'll be in and out of the manufacturing floor."

Gulping down her concerns, she nodded.

He led her through the busy manufacturing area, explaining each process and introducing her to the employees, including a massive security officer who looked like a professional bodybuilder. Thankfully, everyone wore a name tag. Otherwise, she'd never remember anyone's name. She still didn't know what to do and was already overwhelmed.

Mr. Lawson dropped her off with the human resource manager.

"Welcome to the company. I'm Kathy Thompson." A

woman with a flawless, milk-chocolate complexion and sparkling brown eyes motioned for Marie to sit at a table. "We have a few items to complete before you start working." Kathy handed her a stack of paperwork to fill out for insurance, forms for the company, and forms on top of forms, along with information about her job assignment that seemed to range from accounting clerk to financial analyst. Kathy explained each one, then left Marie alone to complete the documents.

Grateful for the privacy to figure everything out, Marie scrolled through her phone to a hidden file where Mr. Smith had left her new social security number, insurance, and other needed data. She paused before she signed the bottom of a document stating that all information she entered was true and correct. Based on past and recent events, it was true. Her degree was the same, even her past job experience, except with her new name.

Finally finished, she looked around Kathy's neat and tidy office. Diplomas hung on the wall, and on the credenza behind her desk were photos of Kathy with children and what must be her husband.

"All done?" Kathy stepped back into her office and took the stack of forms. "Let's get you situated." She took Marie back to her office. "Everything should be ready for you. Mrs. Box retired a few weeks ago but left notes about the job. She'd planned on being available to help with her replacement's transition, but her husband surprised her with a trip to Paris. It might only be Paris, Texas, but it still was a trip," she chuckled. "Plus, Trudi knows how things are done. She works at the front desk, but I think she's up to speed on almost every job in the facility. We like to help each other out around here, so don't hesitate to ask."

Marie thanked Kathy, settled in her desk, and picked up the first folder. She couldn't believe the detail Mrs. Box had left for her. Her notes were simple, easy to follow, and even had little smiley faces.

"How are you doing?" Trudi Lawson stopped in front of Marie's desk. "Any questions?"

"I think I'm figuring everything out. Mrs. Box did an amazing job with her notes."

"She is fun, crazy, wild, and meticulous. She'll probably drop in to say hello once she returns from her travels. Have you had a chance to explore the town?"

Marie nodded. "I've looked around a few of the streets."

"If you see the big Tudor house with lots of flowers, that's the one that belongs to Mrs. Box and her husband. Her landscaping has won the town's beautification award almost every year."

"I did see her house. It's beautiful."

"Isn't it, though? I wish I had her green thumb. When she gets back, make sure you ask her if you can drop by. The front yard is beautiful, but her backyard is even more spectacular. It's what gardening magazines would want on their covers."

"I thought that when I looked at her yard."

"Do you like to garden?" Trudi asked.

"Yes, my Abuela had beautiful flowers." Her grandmother had lovingly tended their tiny yard, creating a haven of beauty in an ugly neighborhood.

"Will your grandmother be coming to visit you?"

If only. "No, she's in heaven."

Trudi placed her gentle hand on Marie's arm. "Oh, I'm so sorry for your loss, but just think she's seeing the most amazing gardens ever."

"I guess she is." Marie sat back in her chair after Trudi left. What a sweet idea to think of her grandmother walking in the perfect heavenly gardens. The thought gave comfort and yet made her a little sad. If only she could see Abuela and her parents again. Thankfully, based on her time with God last night, she had the comfort of knowing they would all be together again one day.

Turning back to her computer, Marie continued working. The more she read about her job responsibilities, the more it seemed tailor-made for her since her degree was in business and accounting.

"Yo, Marie!" Alexa, the girl with the lightning bolt in her hair, zipped into her office. "Ready for lunch?"

Marie glanced at the time. She couldn't believe four hours had passed since she'd arrived. "Sure. Do I need to tell anyone I'm leaving?"

"No worries, I've already let Trudi know. Come on. Grace is already in the car."

Marie signed off the computer, put away the folders, and followed Alexa outside.

They piled inside Grace's immaculate four-door sedan. Grace drove the exact speed limit as Alexa chatted about a bad date she had the night before.

"The guy wasn't my type," Alexa explained. "Even Grace,

with her brainy calculations, hasn't figured out my type."

Grace let out a loud sigh. "It truly is a problem without a solution."

Marie followed Grace and Alexa into Tiddlywinks and sat across the table. For a small town, the restaurant seemed always to be busy.

Alexa glanced at the menu and then leaned toward Marie. "So, what brings you to Crawdadville?"

"I needed a new start," Marie said. It was the truth.

Alexa tilted her head, narrowed her eyes, then sat back in her chair and nodded. "Good enough."

Marie turned her attention from Alexa's scrutiny to Grace. "How about you both? What brought you to Crawdad Beach?"

"I grew up here, moved away to attend college, then came back to work." Grace's voice was quiet, timid, as though she hated bringing attention to herself. "My dad and his wife moved last year to the Hamptons." Her reaction seemed mixed with that final statement.

"Grace's family used to live in that big brick house with the columns," Alexa said. "I moved here with the job, wanted to be close to the beach but not too close when a hurricane or storm hits. At least here we are five hundred feet above sea level."

"Hi, y'all!" The waitress, Jennifer, brought glasses of water and stood next to their table. "Marie, did you enjoy your lunch with David?" Jennifer's eyebrows playfully shimmied.

Heat rocketing up Marie's neck and cheeks, she nodded.

"David Mitchell?" Alexa shot a curious look at Marie. "You've been holding out on us, haven't you?"

"I'd be after him myself if I weren't already engaged," Jennifer said. "What can I get y'all?"

After Jennifer took their orders, Alexa turned her attention back to Marie. "So, you and David? He's a hottie and one of the most eligible bachelors in town. How did you meet him?"

"At the grocery store," she mumbled.

Alexa sat there for a moment, surveying her. "Well, I can see that. You would make a cute couple. Don't you think so, Grace?"

Her friend studied Marie. "Definitely. I'd say there would be a 96.78 percent probability of an attraction."

Alexa motioned with her chin. "She's into numbers, calculates all kinds of stuff in that brainy head of hers."

Grace blushed, hung her head, but grinned.

"So, Marie, do you like to run?" Alexa asked.

"Only when necessary. "

"Well, everybody is running from something. So, where you living?"

"I'm in a duplex."

Grace nodded. "The Bowman's place."

Marie sipped her water. Everyone seemed to know everyone in town and know everything about everyone. Hopefully, that would be a good thing and not a negative.

"Grace and I are roommates," Alexa said. "We live in the lofts in the old bank building on main street. It's a cool setup. We both have a bedroom with an ensuite bathroom, and the den and kitchen are in the middle. You'll have to stop by after work one day, and we'll show you around."

"Thanks. That would be nice."

"Have you been by the antique store?" Grace asked. "They have great items, some big and pricey, but others are good for those on a budget."

"You've got to visit Doohickeys, " Alexa added.

Marie looked back and forth between them. "I haven't made it to either place. I hope to go this next weekend."

"Okay, it's a plan," Alexa said. "Stop by our place around nine thirty on Saturday." She took out her phone. "We'll exchange numbers. Text or call anytime."

During lunch, they continued talking and laughing like Marie had always been part of their friendship. She could get used to having instant friends.

Back at work, she continued following the instructions left by Mrs. Box. Data needed to be entered, and Marie couldn't believe how everything flowed so easily. Concentrating on her work, she sensed movement.

A blond, overly-tanned man about six feet tall walked into her office and stood in front of her desk. "Hey there, beautiful. So, you're the new girl. I'm Max." His words had an over-the-top confidence. "You sure are a nice change from frumpy old Mrs. Box." His gaze roamed from her face to her chest.

Seemingly, out of nowhere, Alexa dashed into the room. "You need to stop bothering her."

Max's massive gold watch flashed in the light as he held up his hands. "Hey, I'm just introducing myself to the new gal."

Alexa huffed. "Gal? She's a woman." She wagged her finger in his face. "I know what you're doing. Marie already has a boyfriend, so just take your conceited self right back to your own office. "

His smile bordering on a hungry wolf, Max gave Marie a side-eye glance. "If you ever want a *good* time, I'll be across the hall."

After he left, Alexa closed Marie's door then zipped next to her. "Avoid him at all costs. We think he has tried to sleep with every woman in a hundred-mile radius."

"Thanks for covering for me, but I don't think it would have stopped him even if I had a boyfriend."

"Well, we need to keep you from the evil clutches of Maximus, the wanna-be-magnificent. The man is a legend in his own mind. Just whistle if you need me." Her head tilted. "Can you whistle?"

Marie attempted but only let out a little twirp of a sound.

"Well, that will do. I'll keep my super-sonic hearing open for anything that sounds like a dying bird." Alexa was out of the door in a flash.

Marie sat back in her chair. She'd dealt with guys like Max, but using her martial arts skills to take care of the situation might be frowned upon by management. However, Alexa would probably cheer her on.

Chuckling, Marie got back to work.

An hour later, she stood and stretched her back. Needing a bathroom break, she stepped into the hall.

Max blocked her path as his gaze traveled across her

body. His mouth twisted into the epitome of smarminess. "We were rudely interrupted earlier." His breath had a slight scent of alcohol. "You're one fine-looking woman. What do you like to do for fun?"

His lewd looks made her want to pour sanitizer over her body. Maybe she could redirect his lustful thoughts. "I like hanging out with friends and going to church."

"Church?" He sneered. "There's nothing fun about church." He leaned closer, his strong cologne gagging her. "I'll show you a *really* good time."

"Max!" Alexa bolted down the hall and tried to get between them. "Get back, you lecherous leech."

"You can't talk to me like that."

"Oh, yeah." Alexa raised her chin and stood taller. "Well, I just did." The shaved part of her lightning bolt reddened as she punched the air with her finger. "If you would act like a gentleman, you might get further with the ladies."

He puffed out his chest and raised his nose in the air. "I get along just fine with the ladies."

"Ha. They're probably *not* ladies if you get along fine with them."

"I resent that." Max's face flamed red. "You're the one who needs to back off. I was just trying to have a nice conversation with Marie."

Alexa put her hands on her hips. "No, you were harassing her."

"What's it to you anyway? This is none of your business. Who promoted you to morality police?" He pushed Alexa hard enough that she hit the wall.

Max then turned to Marie. "Let me show you a good time." He vice-gripped her arm and pulled her against him, one hand settling on her rear end.

Chapter 14

Flaming mad, Marie's primal instincts kicked in, jerking her leg up, she connected with an area that brought him to his knees.

As Max writhed on the floor whimpering, she leaned down. "If you *ever* try anything like that again, crying will be the least of your worries."

Alexa' stood with her mouth gaping open.

Marie glared at Max before grinning at Alexa. "Maybe I should have mentioned that I'm a black belt. I actually went easy on him."

Dancing, Alexa followed Marie into her office. "Girl, you're the woman! Kudos, kudos, kudos. And I thought I needed to protect you. Oh, man, we're going to have fun together."

Marie sat at her desk and looked up at her new friend. "What a way to start my first day. Do you think I'll get in trouble?" Even though she was only defending herself, she was the new person, and she did knee a guy in the groin. She had far too much practice in that technique to protect herself in her old neighborhood,

Alexa perched on the edge of Marie's desk. "Trouble? For defending yourself? No way. You might get a medal from every female employee in the place."

"Is Max always like that?"

"He's usually not that bad. But he's always worse when the Lawson's or HR isn't looking. He thinks he's a lady's man, but he went too far this time. I think the only reason he's still with the company is because he's one heck of a salesman."

"It doesn't seem right to keep somebody that harasses women. Should I say something to Human Resources?"

"Definitely. I reported him last week for coming on to a new girl working out on the floor. Kathy in Human Resources did talk to Max, but since he didn't touch her, they just gave him a warning. But today. This was wrong. He pushed me, and he grabbed you in ways that are *never* appropriate."

Marie nodded and stood to her feet. "I'll go talk to Kathy."

Alexa rubbed her hands together. "I'll come with you since I was a witness."

As they neared the HR office, she could hear Max's voice. "She attacked me. I want you to fire her!"

Alexa banged open the door and bolted toward Max. "I was there and saw what happened. He pushed me against the wall, and then he grabbed Marie. She was only defending herself."

Kathy glared at Max. "Is that true?"

He cleared his throat. "I might have gently touched her arm."

"Gently?" Alexa huffed. "He grabbed her, pulled her against his body, and put his hand on her ... tushy, her bottom, uh, her rear end!"

Marie showed Kathy her arm where bruises were already forming from where he gripped her arm.

Kathy picked up her phone. "To my office. STAT."

Moving toward the door, Max cursed under his breath and lasered them all with a glare that could charbroil a steak. Before he could exit, the massive security officer towered over Max, stopping his forward progress.

Kathy nodded toward the man. "Escort Max to his office and stay with him until I call. Make sure he doesn't talk to anyone until I have a chance to interview him."

As the officer led Max out, Kathy turned her attention to Marie. "I'd like to talk to you first. Alexa, please go to your cubicle. The same rule applies to you. No talking to anyone until I call for you."

Two hours later, Marie sat at her desk and rubbed her forehead. HR and the security guy had interviewed her. On her first day at work, she'd had to defend herself against an assaulting employee. What a way to make a first impression. So much for living a quiet life and staying out of the spotlight.

She surveyed the medal Alexa had made for her using the company's 3-D printer that read *Heroic Defender of the Lawson women.*

Marie didn't feel like a hero. Max had been fired, and she'd been cleared of any wrongdoing, but she felt sick to her stomach.

"You okay?" Wide-eyed Grace stood at her doorway. "Alexa told me what happened."

"Yeah, I'm fine, but it's been an interesting first day."

Grace moved in front of her desk. "I'm sorry. It was brave of you to stand up against Max."

"I feel bad that he lost his job."

"Don't. He did that to himself. Marie, he's been making women around here miserable for quite some time. Usually, he's just flirty, but today, his actions went to a new, frightening level. We're behind you. I'm sorry it happened. I hope you enjoy working here."

"Thanks. Me too."

Mr. Lawson and Kathy knocked on the open door. "May we come in?"

At Marie's nod, they entered as Grace excused herself.

The big man's gentle eyes showed genuine compassion. "Marie, we're sorry about Max's actions toward you, and I'm angry you were put in that situation. We will be making sure we have the proper procedures and policies so something like this does *not* happen again. I, and this company, will do everything we can to ensure this working environment is safe. We are grateful you're here, Marie. Please let me, Trudi, Kathy, security, or any of us know if you need anything. Okay?"

"Thank you, Mr. Lawson. Thank you, Kathy." As they left, Marie swiped at the moisture building in her eyes.

Releasing the tension in her shoulders, she sat back in her chair. Well, if this was her first day, maybe she'd gotten through the worst. Surely, things would be less eventful.

Chapter 15

Saturday morning, Marie walked along the sidewalk on Main Street. Besides the incident with Max, her first week at work had gone better than expected. She enjoyed the job and getting to know her co-workers.

Marie entered the converted bank building and knocked on the door of her new friend's apartment.

"Welcome to our home. What do you think?" Her lightning bolt friend, Alexa, dressed in jean shorts and a florescent pink top, waved her hand like a game show hostess as Marie entered. "We moved in last year. It's been great living downtown and close to work. David Mitchell's mom is the renovator and designer of the loft apartments." Alexa gave an approving glance around their place. "She's working on another building down the street."

"I love it." Marie couldn't believe how cute their apartment was, with high ceilings, an open and airy layout, exposed beams and ductwork, and large windows that let in plenty of natural light. The furniture was a mix of new and old, creating a look of whimsy comfort. They even had a balcony overlooking the main street.

Grace, wearing khaki-colored shorts and a muted green blouse, followed as Alexa led Marie around their place. Grace's neat room had a bed, dresser, desk, a computer with two screens, headphones, a microphone, and recording equipment.

Alexa pointed to the desk. "Grace makes music on the side. Her songs have even charted."

Marie glanced at Grace. "Really? I'm impressed."

Grace pushed her glasses up on her nose and shrugged. "It's just something fun to do when I'm not working."

"I'll send you the links so you can listen," Alexa got out her phone. "Even though her music is awesome, her dad and stepmom disapprove. They wanted her to be a surgeon, so Grace uses an alias online. Only a few people know her pseudo name."

"Pseudonym," Grace corrected.

"Nah, it's a pseudo name. It's not you, but it's you."

Marie grinned at their banter. "Whatever alias you're using, I'm looking forward to listening."

Grace gave her a shy smile. "Thank you."

Alexa motioned for Marie to follow her to her room. Posters of track stars lined the walls, and the bed and floor looked like a clothing bomb had exploded.

Apartment tour over, Alexa led them down the street to Knick Knacks Antique store. The older building was crowded with furniture, glassware, antique jewelry, art, old toys, and a variety of items.

A woman with short silver hair sat reading behind a long counter. She glanced up and smiled. "Please let me know if I can help you find anything."

"Thank you, Mrs. Bounds," Grace said, then pointed. "This is Marie. She just moved here."

Mrs. Bounds' kind, hazel-eyed gaze traveled her way. "Nice to meet you. Did you move into the Bowman place?"

"Yes." She might as well wear a sign on her forehead.

"Welcome to Crawdad Beach."

"Thank you. I'm enjoying living here." Other than a few people, the sentiment was genuine.

"I'm so glad," Mrs. Bounds said. "We kind of like it too. I believe you've met my brother. Mr. Doss. He lives on your street."

Marie gave her a big smile. "Yes, he's such a nice man."

"Any new stuff this week?" Alexa asked.

"I think I have something you'll really like." Mrs. Bounds grinned and pointed to the toy section.

"Woot!" Alexa ran toward where the woman directed.

Mrs. Bounds directed her gaze back to her. "Marie, I'm grateful to make your acquaintance. Maybe I'll see you when I visit my brother."

"That would be nice." Marie excused herself and walked to the back to survey bookshelves crowded with used books. Hardback copies of old English novels caught her attention. Besides the contemporary suspense books she liked reading, it would be fun to escape back in time.

"Do you like to read?" Grace fingered an old book as she stood next to her.

"Yes, suspense or mystery."

Grace leaned close as a blush rose to her cheeks. "I like historical, especially Westerns." Her voice was a mere whisper.

"Really?" Marie figured Grace would read scientific

textbooks since she was always spouting off statistics.

"Yes, I'd be out west in a mountain cabin. A homestead of my own with several horses, and I'd be a crack shot." Grace shot with her finger and blew out her imaginary barrel. "How about you? If you were a character in a book, where would you go? What would you be?"

"I'd be a smart, savvy, international spy with superpowers. There's something freeing about living through a fictional character who always triumphs no matter how difficult their journey." If only she could write herself into a novel, she'd make sure the killer was caught, and she'd get a happy-ever-after ending.

"I can see that." Grace studied her for a moment. "Definitely. Well, you might not be a super spy, but you have a story."

Marie felt the blood rush from her face.

Grace's head tilted as she continued to survey her. "Crawdad Beach and Lawson Manufacturing will be good places for you. Don't worry. Whatever brought you here will be good, you will triumph." Grace smiled and walked away.

A shiver ran up her spine as she stood there, trying to figure out what happened. Did Grace know something about Marie's situation, or was Grace just a supersmart person who figured things out?

Alexa zipped toward her and screeched to a stop. "What did Grace say to you? You look like you've seen a ghost."

"It was nothing." Marie gripped the books she'd found to her chest.

"Yeah, right. I bet she gave you another one of her

probability things. She's amazing with her predictions." Alexa shrugged and then held up a poster with a cartoon roadrunner. "I love this guy. He was always outwitting the coyote." She laughed, then glanced at the books Marie had in her hand. "Pay up. We're heading next to Doohickeys. I need to buy a few things to hang some more posters."

After paying for their purchases, Marie followed behind her friends. What a strange combination those two made, and the fact they welcomed her into their wacky friendship made it even more fun.

Wood floors creaked in greeting as they entered Doohickey's Hardware Store. The ceiling looked like the original tin, and the walls were covered in deep, rich wood shelving seemingly frozen in time from the early 1900s. Some items crammed on the numerous shelves looked to have been there for years, and others were brand new.

"I love this place." Grace took a deep breath. "How many people came here looking to fix and improve their homes and property?" She motioned for Marie to follow and stopped at a display on the back wall of old farm and house implements displayed in huge glass cases. "Think about all the people looking to build a new life who came here. Others are now restoring the old houses." She turned her attention to Marie. "You said you came here because you needed a new start. Are you building new or restoring?"

"Well," Marie took a breath. "I guess building new." And maybe someday God would restore all that she'd lost.

"Nice." Grace pushed her glasses further up her nose. "Someday, I'd like to do that." She turned and walked away.

Marie stood there examining the antique items. Did Grace feel trapped in her hometown? It seemed like she wanted to fade into the background and not bring attention to herself.

A teenage salesclerk did a double take, eyes wide with admiration as Grace walked past him, then hurried to catch up to her. "Can I help you find anything?"

Grace's gaze dropped to the floor. "No, thank you. I'm just looking."

"Yo, Sammie. I could use your help." Alexa, from the end of the aisle, called to the teenager.

The young guy cast a longing glance at Grace before he walked toward Alexa.

Marie wandered through the store. Did Grace even have any idea how attractive she was? Why would someone as intelligent as Grace have a difficult time making a new start? Marie rubbed the back of her neck. She was one to talk. If she hadn't been taken into protective custody, she'd probably still be living in the town where she grew up, or worse yet dead.

Alexa skipped toward them. "Hey, let's stop by the store so I can pick up some things for lunch. I'm in the mood to make something." Her gaze stopped at Marie. "You're staying for lunch, right?"

"Sure. That would be nice, thank you." And visiting the store might give her the chance to see David.

Grace leaned close as they made their way to the car. "Alexa is a fabulous chef. She can whip up some pretty interesting dishes."

"Really?" Marie didn't hide her surprise. She couldn't

imagine Alexa doing anything but moving fast. Curiosity piqued, Marie followed her friends to their next destination.

At the grocery store, Alexa zoomed down the aisles and threw items in her cart.

Marie chuckled. How could she create anything appetizing from those choices?

Alexa screeched to a stop in the produce section and stared at a big, muscular male store employee carrying a box of watermelons on his shoulders. She whistled. "Looking fine there, Tony."

The big guy stopped, his face flamed crimson, and his big mustache twitched. "Alexa." His voice held a level of awe.

Alexa stood still, just grinning.

With slow, deliberate steps, Tony set down the crate and moved closer to her, then stopped, seemingly frozen in place. Beads of sweat popped on his forehead.

Grace nudged Marie. "This is the first time Tony has made a move toward Alexa." She whispered. "I've always wondered about Alexa's type. Now, I see. Opposites attract. There's a 97.54 percent probability they will get together."

Marie stifled a giggle as the standoff continued.

An eyebrow rose on Alexa's face as though daring the big man to come closer.

Tony gulped but didn't move.

"Should we do something?" Marie whispered to Grace.

"Yes, be still and watch. Just think of it like those nature shows. The hunter and the hunted. Alexa is the lion. Poor Tony doesn't have a chance."

The big man gulped, took another step toward her.

"Tony, there you are." A young, attractive, blonde woman Marie recognized as one of the store's cashiers walked toward him. "Could you check in the storeroom for white cake mix? Ms. Tiffany needs some."

The spell broken, Tony snapped to attention. "Sure, I'd be glad to." He gave a longing glance at Alexa, then hurried to the back of the store.

Alexa shrugged and let out a long sigh.

"The prey escapes," Grace whispered.

David focused on his house's wall painting project. His ears tuned to an audible Sherlock Holmes book. The detective mastermind never failed to solve whatever mystery came his way. David stepped back to check his work. Even a second coat of paint on the wall didn't hide the original pink color or, as his sister had explained, fuchsia color.

He probably should have used a primer like the guys at Doohickey's Hardware had suggested. Maybe he should buy a paint gun. Blasting paint on the walls would be more fun than using a roller and paintbrush.

His doorbell rang, and his front door opened. "David?" Tony's voice came from down the hall.

"In the back bedroom." David set down his paint roller and turned off the audible book.

Tony shoved his big hands into his jean's pockets. "Got a minute?"

"Yes, my dear man. How can I help?"

"I'm on break. I'll head back to the store in a few. Everything is fine. I need advice." Tony's face contorted as though in pain. "Woman advice."

"Ah, how can I be of assistance." David envisioned himself as the great detective studying his friend.

"You know I have dating issues. My last attempt was a miserable failure, but now Alexa came into the store."

David blinked for a few minutes. If only he had a pipe like Sherlock Holmes, he could chew on it as he pondered. "Okay?"

Tony's face flamed red, and he swallowed hard. "She's hot."

"Hot as in the day is hot, or hot as in..." Understanding dawned. David wanted to smack himself on the forehead. Good grief, he was slow. Did Tony like Alexa? What an odd combination. Then again, slow and steady Tony could probably mesh with speedy Alexa. Maybe that would work. "So, old chap, you like the girl. That's good."

Tony shook his head. "No."

"No? I'm afraid I'm not following you."

"It's not good." Tony paced back and forth. "I mean, it's good, but what would she see in a guy like me? She's hot, and you know she has that cool lightning thing shaved in her head. I'm just normal."

"Normal?" David chuckled, then reigned in his humor as he surveyed his panicked friend. "Tony, you're a great guy. You're strong and handsome. I mean, you're not my type, but I've heard women say that about you. That you're hot, you know?" What an awkward thing to say to a friend. Sherlock

Holmes would not be impressed.

"Really?"

David nodded. "Perhaps ask Alexa on a date and see how things progress."

"A date?" Tony's eyes rounded. "A date." He stilled. "Maybe that would work. But where would I take someone like her? I don't have a clue what she likes."

"Well, most girls eat and like to eat. Therefore, my dear fellow, ask her to go with you to a restaurant for a nice dinner."

"I can do that. But I don't have her number. So, do I just have to wait in the store and hope I see her again?"

"Ah, I see your dilemma, my good chap." David bucked himself up. He could do this, be the detective. "I believe Marie works with Alexa. Perhaps I could question her and find out if she has the number of her co-worker." Such excellent advice if he didn't say so himself. Tony would be happy, and he would have an opportunity to call Marie.

The color returned to Tony's face. "You'd do that for me?"

David gave a nod. "Yes, my dear chap. I'll get to it soon and let you know."

"That'd be great. Thanks." Tony's eyes narrowed as he gazed at his friend. "But, why do you keep talking so strange and in a pitiful English accent?

Heat crawled up David's neck. "Sorry, I've been listening to audible Sherlock Holmes books set in old England. I'm on my second one this morning."

"Makes sense. I thought maybe the paint fumes got to you

or something. I better get back to work. Thanks for the advice."

"You are most welcome. Stop by anytime." David grinned to himself. The great detective had come up with a most excellent idea. He'd ring up the fair maiden, Marie, and ask for Alexa's information.

His thoughts screeched to a stop. Calling a girl and asking a girl for the number of another girl was probably the worst idea ever. Good grief. He'd have to be delicate in handling the matter and ensure Marie knew Alexa's number wasn't for him but for Tony.

Chewing on his dilemma, David switched back on his audible mystery. Perhaps listening further to Sherlock would get his brain juices flowing in the right direction.

Chapter 16

Back at her place, Marie finished laundry and cleaned her apartment. The interesting meal Alexa prepared had been surprisingly good. Once they finished, they sat around discussing topics like Marie had always been part of their friendship.

Plopping on the couch, she picked up one of the books she'd bought at the antique store.

Three chapters into the story, she stopped for a break. Good thing she was reading the novel on the weekend, or she'd be breaking out in old English. She grinned as she tried speaking like someone from hundreds of years ago. "The day passed pleasantly with playful and lively conversations with her companions, she then returned to her humble abode in good spirits. For truly forsooth, living in the town hath been a pleasant experience."

Hearing a whimpering, she stepped out on her back patio to water her flowers.

Tail wagging, Mr. Doss's dog stood outside her screen door.

"Hey, Filbert. What are you doing here?"

The little dog barked, then trotted away.

Concerned that something might have happened to Mr. Doss, Marie hurried to his house.

Fortunately, her elderly friend seemed fine as he picked up fallen magnolia leaves. Filbert stood beside him, wagging his tail as she walked toward them.

Marie picked up a leaf and tossed it into Mr. Doss's bag. "It's a never-ending battle, isn't it?"

"Yes." Mr. Doss smiled her way. "The tree seems to lose a few daily and yet thrives. How are you today?"

"I'm doing well, thank you. Filbert came to get me."

"He did?" He grinned at his furry friend. "I'm sorry that may have been my fault. I was just talking to him about you."

"You were?" How funny that he'd been discussing her with his dog. For some reason, it seemed to make sense.

"Yes, I told him we needed to see how you were doing. Evidently, he took it upon himself to drop in on you."

She chuckled as she patted the little dog on the head. "Well, aren't you a smart little thing?"

Filbert wagged, then rolled over for a belly rub.

"I believe he's taken a shine to you," Mr. Doss said. "Our furry companions can be quite a blessing." His gaze went from Filbert to her. "So, what have you been up to lately?"

"I started a new job at Lawson Manufacturing."

"Good for you. That's a good company. The owners are charming people."

"That's kind of what David said."

One of Mr. Doss's eyebrows raised. "David?"

"David Mitchell. He works at the grocery store."

"Ah, I'm familiar with the young man." Mr. Doss's eyes twinkled as he grinned. "He's special."

"He is." Just thinking about him made heat rise to her

cheeks. "I forget everyone seems to know everyone in this town."

Mr. Doss chuckled. "Most of the time that's a blessing. Would you join me for a glass of lemonade?"

"That would be nice, thank you."

He motioned for her to sit on the bench under the big oak tree, then went inside, leaving her and Filbert seated in the shade. The little dog tilted his head as he studied her, then, with a wag, turned his attention back to the yard as though monitoring the street.

Maybe she needed to get a dog. It would be nice to have a fur friend. She could get one small enough to sit on her lap but big enough to be a protector. Then again, the little chihuahua, Paco, that had lived next door to Abuela could have probably done more damage than a Doberman. Paco might have been tiny, but he had a huge attitude. Her ankle still had a few scars from a run-in with him.

"Here you go." Mr. Doss handed her a glass and sat next to her.

She thanked him and enjoyed the cool, tart, but sweet drink. Although the temperature was warm, puffy clouds and a gentle breeze kept the air mild and agreeable.

"Are you settling in here in Crawdad Beach?"

"Yes, I'm enjoying the town and the people."

"That's good to hear. I am quite fond of both. Would you be able to perhaps stay for dinner this evening? Family is dropping by, and I'd love for you to meet them."

Marie paused. "I wouldn't want to intrude."

"It would be a blessing for us all if you would join us."

Although the thought made her nervous, how could she say no to such a kind and gentle man? "Thank you. Can I bring anything?"

"Just bring yourself. We always have plenty, and our gatherings are casual." Mr. Doss glanced at his watch and picked up his cane that leaned against the bench. "I better be prepared." He motioned with his chin as an SUV drove toward them. "That's my son-in-law now."

Marie stood next to Mr. Doss as the vehicle parked in his driveway.

A dark-haired man with graying temples took a casserole dish from the backseat and walked toward them. "Katherine is running late, so she asked me to come on over and bring what she'd prepared. She should be here shortly."

Mr. Doss turned to Marie. "I'd like to introduce you to my son-in-law, Michael. Michael, this is Marie. She's new to our area. She's joining us for dinner."

"Good to meet you." He smiled. "Let me drop this off, and I'll come back and join you."

Wagging and jumping, Filbert followed the man into the house.

A white pickup truck pulled into the driveway, and an attractive woman with dark hair walked toward them. "Hi, Dad. I see Michael made it."

"He just went inside. Katherine, I'd like to introduce you to Marie. She recently moved into the Bowman's duplex."

Katherine smothered Marie in a big hug. "It's so nice to meet you."

Surprised at the affection, Marie half-stumbled back after

the embrace. "Nice to meet you, too."

"Sorry about that, I'm a hugger." Katherine embraced her dad. "How are you doing?"

Mr. Doss grinned. "I've been taking care of myself while you've been away."

"You better." Katherine nudged him with her elbow. "Or, I'll tell the doc on you." She turned to Marie. "Dad had his hip replaced, so we keep a sharp eye on him. Plus, he had some heart problems and has a sweet tooth. I caught him one time eating almost a whole package of cookies."

Mr. Doss leaned against his cane as he grinned at Marie.

"Hey, Katherine." Michael stood on the front steps. "What temperature should I set the oven?"

"225 just to keep it warm." Katherine turned to Marie. "I better get inside and help." She left Marie standing next to Mr. Doss.

"My wife was Asian," he said. "I noticed the curiosity in your gaze." He smiled at Marie. "My wife was a beautiful woman inside and out. Katherine takes after her mother."

Laughter came inside the house as Marie followed Mr. Doss. The simple furniture looked older but in good condition. Hardwood floors, and family photos were throughout the house, along with a basket of toys and even a little bed for Filbert.

The front door flew open, and a little boy and girl rushed inside and grabbed Mr. Doss's legs. "Poppa D!"

The smile on Mr. Doss's face erased all his wrinkles as he knelt and hugged them. "Hey, kiddos!"

A young woman, probably in her 30s, with long brown

hair and beautiful almond-shaped eyes, carrying a casserole dish, followed behind. "Poppa D, how ya be?"

He chuckled as he hugged her. "I'm great."

"I'm sorry Paul isn't here," the young woman said. "You know how it is. He's always on the road. He should be in later tonight from his latest business trip. Has my baby brother arrived? He's bringing the meat."

"Not yet. Please let me introduce you to our guest. This is Marie Delgado. She recently moved here."

"It's nice to meet you. Are you the one living at the Bowman place?"

"That's me," Marie grinned.

The children hurried toward the toy box, with Filbert wagging and following behind.

"Hello!" Carrying a cake, the lady from the antique store walked toward them and set the dessert on the kitchen counter. "Marie, I'm so glad you're here."

Mr. Doss hugged the woman. "I take it you've met my sister, Helen."

"Yes," Marie said. "You work at the antique store, right? It's a great store."

"Thank you. My husband's aunt left it to us when she passed away. I'm always grateful when we get a new client. I think you chose some novels."

"Yes, it's been fun to immerse in a tale from England with castles, damsels in distress, and dashing heroes."

Helen chuckled. "They are a fun escape, aren't they?"

The front door opened with a thump. "Hey, can I get a hand?"

Wanting to help, Marie ran down the hall and stared into the face of David Mitchell.

Chapter 17

"Egad!" Wide-eyed, David stumbled back as he juggled the armload of food.

"Forsooth!" Marie's face blazed hot. Why did she have to read that old novel with its old English sayings?

"Did you just say forsooth?" David doubled over in laughter, almost dropping what he was carrying.

She burst out in a laugh as she helped him with the food. "Hey, you started it with Egad."

"Sorry about the egad. It wasn't you." David chuckled as he struggled to compose himself. "I've been listening to audible versions of the original Sherlock Holmes books."

"I understand." Marie wiped the laughter tears as she nodded. "I blame the old English novel I'm reading."

"What are you doing here? I mean, wow, it's awesome to see you."

"It's great to see you too. Mr. Doss invited me."

"You know Grandad?" David shifted to look inside the house, then back to her.

Marie closed her open mouth. "Mr. Doss is your grandfather?" So much for her skill at being aware of her surroundings. How could she have missed the connection?

Smiling, David's sister walked toward them. "You two know one another?"

"Yeah." David nodded. "Marie just moved here. Tess, you've met Marie. Marie, this is my sister Tess."

"I've had the pleasure," Tess grinned at Marie, then turned to David. "Here, I'll take the food, so you two can egad and forsooth all you'd like." Laughing, she took the tray and left them in the front hall.

"It's great you're here." David motioned for Marie to follow him inside. "Have you met my parents?"

"I did, but I didn't realize you were all related."

"Small world, huh? I should have known you'd met Grandad since you live on his street."

"Uncle David!" His nephew and niece ran and jumped into his arms. He smothered them both in hugs and kisses. "Emily and Eric, you've met Ms. Marie, right?"

"Yes," Emily said. "She's pretty."

Eric's cheeks turned bright red. "She's real pretty."

"I agree." David grinned at Marie. "She is very beautiful."

Heat blazing her face, Marie grinned.

Laughter and fun conversation filled the evening. David's parents recounted the fun things they'd experienced and seen on their most recent road trip. Tess shared humorous stories about her children. Mr. Doss's sister said something funny that happened at her store. David chuckled about the toddler who ran wild in the grocery. Even Mr. Doss shared a funny story about Filbert.

Even though Marie didn't add much to the conversation, she never felt left out. They welcomed her like she'd been a part of their family for years.

Tess laughed as she told a cute story about David when

he was younger.

Eyes narrow but grinning, David put down his sandwich. "Oh, come on. I was only three at the time."

"It was the funniest thing." Tess giggled as she smiled at Marie. "You should have seen him standing there covered in mud."

David's mom joined in the laughter. "It took me over an hour to scrub him clean. I've never seen so much mud covering a human being."

"I think I lost hearing in my left ear for a week." He winced. "Mud everywhere in every crevasse in my body. I'll never know why women pay a spa for a mud bath."

"David was always getting into something," His mom said.

"Really?" Marie glanced his way. "So you were mischievous?"

"Me? No, I was the model child."

Tess snorted. "You? The only model you would be is as a rambunctious, crazy, and wild child."

"Wild child, huh?" Marie giggled.

"Why is everyone picking on me?" David placed his hand on his chest. "I know, as the youngest child in the family, I'm the one everyone picks on. Poor me. Poor little me."

Tess playfully smacked his arm. "Oh, buck it up, little brother. You had a charmed childhood."

David laughed. "I did." He looked at Marie. "I really did. Spoiled rotten and loved every minute of it. How about you? Did you ever get into any mischief?"

Marie tried to think back. "Not too much. But my grandmother said that when I was three, I got mad at her for not letting me have ice cream for breakfast, so I packed my bag and walked out the front door."

"Packed your bag?" David tilted his head. "What did you take? Where were you planning to go?"

"I took a teddy bear, my favorite blanket, and a pair of extra sneakers, and I was going to walk to paradise."

"Paradise? You mean like Hawaii?"

"Nope. Paradise Ice Cream Shop."

David chuckled and gave her a high-five. "Good job. Best story of the evening."

"You win with that one," Mr. Doss said. "And it just so happens the person who tells the best story wins an ice cream cone."

"Really?" Marie leaned closer to David. "Is he kidding?"

"Nope. It's actually one of the things we do when we get together. Whoever tells the best story wins ice cream in the summer and hot chocolate in the winter. Your timing on sharing was perfect."

Perfect. Just perfect. Marie glanced over at David as he walked her home. She couldn't believe what a great time she had with his family.

David bumped her shoulder. "You know, I'm jealous."

She stopped and turned toward him. "What? Why?" Did she do something wrong?

David tossed her a wink. "Eric wouldn't leave you alone. Honestly, the little brut kept you occupied the whole evening. And my parents, my grandad, aunt, *and* my sister gushed and fawned all over you. And me? I was just left there alone, by myself, munching on food, as the family ignored me. Totally ignored me." He nudged her with his elbow. "I'm teasing you. It was a great evening. I couldn't have scripted a better one. Really, Marie, I'm glad you were with us this evening. I was hoping to invite you to a family get-together. Granddad beat me to it."

"Thank you for making me feel so welcome." Not wanting the evening to end, she paused outside her door as the porch light bathed them in a gentle glow.

David stepped close to her, so close his clean scent enveloped her senses. "I'm glad you moved here." He cupped her face with his palms and drew her to him.

Her breath caught, and her cheeks flamed to scorching as he kissed her. Her every hair seemed to raise in awe. She didn't know how long they kissed, only that her head spun when they stopped.

He held her close. "Man, you're the best kisser."

Marie nestled in his arms as his heart pounded in her ears. She tried to gather her scattered, floating thoughts. "I was going to say the same thing about you."

"Thank you, Marie."

She giggled at his comment. "Thank you, David. This was the best night ever."

"I have other skills, you know." He nuzzled and kissed her neck.

Squealing, she broke away. "That tickles."

"So I found your weakness, did I?" Humor danced in his eyes as he stepped close.

Not to be outdone, she quirked an eyebrow. "So, what is

your weakness?" Raising on her tiptoes, she feather-kissed his neck.

David twisted out of her embrace. "Not fair, woman. So, not fair."

"You're ticklish too." Marie laughed.

"I will not admit that." He grinned and rubbed his neck. "Guys aren't ticklish."

"Oh, be a man and admit it. My superhero kisser has a weakness."

"Superhero kisser, huh?" David stood tall and puffed out his chest.

"Don't let it go to your head." She playfully punched him.

He drew her close and kissed her again. With a moan, he stepped back. "I better go. I really better go."

Whew! Marie took out her phone and turned off the alarm. Opening her door, she turned toward him. "See you soon?"

"Definitely." He grinned. "But it won't be soon enough. See you at church in the morning?"

"Oh, right. I guess so."

"Wait!" David held out his hand before she could shut the door. "I forgot to ask you something. Tony asked if you would give Alexa's number to me so I could give it to Tony. It's not for me, you know. I'm not interested in Alexa. I know it's weird to ask a girl for another girl's number." His neck beat red, he clamped his mouth shut and gave her an apologetic grin.

Smiling, she gave him Alexa's information. "That's one connection I'm curious about."

"I know, right? I wouldn't put them together, but you never know." He stepped closer and gave her a quick kiss.

With a happy sigh, she locked herself inside and watched out the front window as David sprinted to his car at his grandad's house. Marie leaned against the window frame as he drove away. She'd never known anyone like David. Plus, he had a fantastic family.

She'd spent most of her life running from, but what would it be like to run to? She'd hidden herself and her heart for so long, maybe it was time to see what would happen in a relationship with David. She took a final look down the street.

Her breath caught. In the shadows, a dark car without headlights drove slowly toward the duplex and stopped with the engine still running.

Chapter 18

Had she been found?

Marie jumped away from the window. She held her breath until the car reversed out of the driveway and drove away. Blowing out air, Marie slammed shut the window blinds. Maybe someone was just driving around, and it was nothing. Perhaps she was just paranoid. But what if it was the bad guy?

Should she call Mr. Smith? What would she say? I saw a car. She raked her hands through her hair. Maybe the car wasn't from her past but instead Max. Did he know where she lived? Would he come after her since he lost his job?

Why couldn't she be like the brave heroine in the novels? She'd have taken her gun, confronted the driver, and asked them what they were doing. But she didn't have a gun, didn't even have a baseball bat. Then again, she was a black belt. Why was she being such a wimp? She could take care of herself.

Straightening her shoulders, she set the alarm and checked the locks on the doors and windows to ensure everything was secure. She had to stop thinking of worst-case scenarios, she'd had a wonderful evening with a wonderful guy, she needed to enjoy her new life.

She'd had a few friends at school and even dated a little

during high school and college, but she always felt the loner, the one left out. Now, she had a chance for friendships and to be part of a family. Maybe not a family with her name, but she'd been welcomed into David's family with open arms.

But how could she be part of any family, especially David's sweet family? If a relationship went further with David, she'd never want to put them in danger.

Awash in a soul-deep craving, longing, a desire for home, family, and a place to belong, she wrapped her arms around herself. Why had Mr. Smith brought her here? Why had God brought her here, just to dangle in front of her something she could never have?

"God, why?" Marie rubbed her eyes. She didn't want to be alone anymore. Why did she always have to be alone? She looked up at the ceiling. "What do I do?" She stood in the silence. Waited.

Trust me.

The words came from inside her, yet outside her. Soft and gentle. She rubbed the goosebumps rising on her arms. Was she imagining things? Would God really speak to her? Jesus, the great Shepherd, said his sheep hear him and would know his voice. God would want her to trust him. Wasn't there a verse about trusting in the Lord? Probably lots of verses about that subject.

She ran to Abuela's Bible, sat on the couch, and thumbed through the pages. Her grandmother had underlined verse after verse about trusting God.

Marie ran her hands through her hair. So, was she supposed to trust God about the car she'd seen or about

David? God probably meant trusting him with everything. Oh, why was that so difficult? Real-life problems were so real and could be such a problem.

"I'm sorry, God. I don't know how to stop worrying about what might happen because I don't know what might happen." Taking a deep breath, she let it out slowly.

Then again, was God in control or not? If he was always in control, why did she need to worry? She didn't know the future, but God did.

Jesus said not to worry about tomorrow and not worry about anything but pray about everything and trust God. She needed to let the worries go, let them all go, and trust God. But that was easier said than done.

Marie got ready for bed and burrowed under her covers with Abuela's Bible nestled in her arms.

"Okay, God. I don't know if I can, but I'll try. Please help me to trust you. Show me, guide me, and help me with this thing with David, whatever this thing might be. And please don't let that car be anything bad."

Six thirty a.m., her alarm screeched. Marie turned it off, rolled over, and threw her pillow over her head. Feeling like she hadn't slept more than a few minutes, she dragged out of bed, drank a giant mug of coffee, and then took a long, hot shower.

All night, she'd worried about the car in her driveway, worried about the possibility of dating David and then having to move again, basically worried about anything and everything. If God gave out report cards, she'd have failed the trust thing.

Her worrying hadn't accomplished anything but rob her of sleep. Maybe she'd hear something at church that would give her some clarity.

Dressed for church, she sat on her patio and ate a breakfast bar. Her phone signaled an incoming text. David messaged how much he enjoyed their time together. She quickly responded with the same sentiments. She'd also had a wonderful time.

His following text made her pause. David asked if she would go on a date with him next Saturday.

Marie stared at his message as all the concerns from her sleepless night tumbled through her thoughts. She still didn't know if she was supposed to trust God to date David or not to date David.

Without replying to his message, she hurried to church.

Fifteen minutes later, she entered the building.

Mr. Doss, his cane in hand, stood by the donut counter. Smiling, he waved. "Good morning. We enjoyed having you over last night."

"Thank you, I had a wonderful time. You have a very special family."

"That I do, and they are a blessing. And as my neighbor and friend, you're officially part of our family now."

Moisture building in her eyes, Marie swallowed the lump rising in her throat. How could she be welcomed that easily into his family? Mr. Doss barely knew her. How could he trust her without reservation? The thoughts made her feel even more guilty about not trusting God.

The music started, and she followed him down the aisle

to a pew closer to the front.

Every song, even the sermon, seemed to be about trusting God. The service ended with an old hymn about trusting and obeying God being the only way to be happy in Jesus.

What would it be like to trust God, let everything go, and enjoy the journey? She wanted that, she really did. Maybe she should wave a white flag, put up her hands, and surrender to God.

"Marie?" Mr. Doss touched her arm.

She blinked and tried to focus. When had the service ended? Most people had already left, and only a few mingled as they talked and visited.

His gentle eyes surveyed her. "Would you like to join us for lunch?"

"I'm not sure. I probably need to take care of a few things before work on Monday."

"Hey, Marie and Grandad." David, all smiles, walked toward them. "Marie, you coming to lunch with us? Mom and Dad are bringing barbecue from the Bodacious Pig. They're the best in the county."

Her traitorous stomach growled loud enough to reverberate off the ceiling.

David chuckled, took her hand, and led her outside.

Did he not even realize she'd ignored his request for a date? Maybe he thought she'd said yes.

Mr. Doss stood beside her in the parking lot and turned to David. "Even though Marie needs to take care of a few things before work tomorrow, I'm sure she'll have time to join us."

He waited until David got in his car, and then his gaze seemed to peer into her soul, the deep crevices of her life she refused to allow others to see, the hopes and dreams that laid dormant for far too long. "I hope you don't mind the little push to join us. We enjoy your company, and you're always welcome. However, if you need to get home, I'll gladly cover for you."

The paranoid part of her wanted to run, but the part that wanted to trust God nudged her forward. "Thank you. I'll be glad to come."

"Good." He took a step, then stopped. "Marie, when my family first adopted me, I wasn't sure I could trust them, and I thought even if I did, something bad might happen. Sometimes, trusting God means letting go of what might happen and trusting God regardless of what does happen. God is loving and trustworthy."

She stood still as he turned and walked away. Did Mr. Doss always seem to read her mind? Or did God just give her the answer to her concerns? If she never took a risk by trusting God, she'd never have the adventure of trusting God.

Marie walked to her car and buckled her seatbelt. The contemporary novel she'd read with the brave heroine came to mind. With risk comes reward, the character would say.

What if she took the chance and dove into her life in the same way? Not so much as a spy or superhero, but as a regular person jumping in with both feet and embracing her new life. She was so tired of living paranoid.

As Marie drove toward her street, the verses about wearing the armor of God came to mind. Now, that sounded like a winning combination. Suited with God's armor, she'd be invincible since, as a Christian, her soul was always safe in Christ, and she'd always get the happy ending.

However, what about keeping her heart safe? If she took a chance on David, maybe she could pray for her heart to have a little suit of armor to keep out hurt and pain and only allow all the good stuff inside. With a smile, she glanced up and sent a prayer to the heavens.

David couldn't stop smiling as he walked Marie home. Lunch had been great with her and his family, "I'm glad you joined us again."

Marie was quiet for a moment. "I've never known a family like yours. You're all so loving toward one another."

"We have our moments and don't always see the same on a few issues, but we try to work things out."

Marie stopped at her front door and turned to him. "Would you like to come in?"

He gave her a hopeful grin. "If you're not too tired of me yet."

Her shy smile tipped his way. "Not yet." She turned off her alarm, unlocked the door, and let him inside. "The Bowmans decorated the place before I got here."

Grateful Marie opened more of her world to him, David took in the surroundings. "It's nice." He didn't see any photos and only a few personal items. A Bible with what looked like a handmade teal cover sat on her coffee table. Did she see the place as temporary, or didn't she have anything she wanted to display?

He pointed toward the coffee table. "I like your Bible."

"It's not mine." She took it in her arms and held it close. "I mean, it is mine now. It used to belong to my grandmother. I never want to be without it."

"Did your grandmother underline and make lots of notes?"

"Yes, she even had dates on some of the passages. I really miss her. It's nice to have something that was so special to her. It's like I still have a part of her with me."

David nodded. "I get that. I hope to have Granddad's Bible if anything happens to him. My sister has my grandmother's Bible. I'm grateful we will see them again. It makes the pain not quite so painful, you know. But it would be nice to call them in heaven."

"That would be nice." Her eyes misty, Marie set the book back on the table. "Want something to drink?" She walked to the kitchen and opened her fridge. "I have water or lemonade that I bought at your store?"

"I'll take a glass of lemonade since you bought the best brand." He wiggled his eyebrows, gaining a smile from her.

She poured them a drink and led him onto her screened-in-covered patio.

He looked past the wicker furniture and the potted flowers on the patio to the manicured backyard filled with blooming plants and crepe myrtles. "This is really nice. What a great view."

"Mrs. Bowman, I mean Julie, spends lots of time keeping it up. I hope she'll let me help her one day," Marie said.

"You like yardwork?"

Marie nodded as she sat in one of the chairs. "Yes. Abuela's yard wasn't big, but it was a little oasis in an ugly neighborhood."

David settled beside her. "I'm sorry about the neighborhood. That must have been tough."

She smiled, but her brow pinched. "It wasn't easy, but Grandmother took good care of me."

"Grandparents can be pretty special."

Marie's gaze went from his to the backyard. "You're fortunate to have Mr. Doss as your Granddad."

"He's a great guy. I'm sorry you didn't meet my grandmother. She was beautiful inside and out with a fun sense of humor."

"Must be nice to have so many happy memories." Her words were only a mumbled whisper.

Sensing her deep wounds, the pain she only partially voiced, David sipped his drink. He'd been blessed with a loving family. They weren't perfect, and sometimes had disagreements, but he always felt loved and safe. The little he knew about Marie spoke volumes of hurt and disappointment.

He leaned toward her. "Maybe God brought you here to make good memories." And, God willing, he hoped he would be one of the best ones, the happy-ever-after kind.

Emotions flitted across her face as her gaze studied him. "That would be nice."

"I'll do my best to help." One elbow leaning on the chair,

he bridged the gap between them and tasted her sweet lips. Her breath quivered as her hand fisted on his shirt, drawing him closer. Wanting to hold her, he shifted.

His elbow slid off, the momentum sending him flailing as the chair slid out from under him. He hit the floor with an embarrassing thump.

Marie jumped to her feet. "Are you okay?"

"Yes, I'm fine." Stifling a groan, he brushed himself off and got to his feet. "However, my pride took a major hit."

With a grin and an eyebrow raised, Marie stepped toward him. "Where does it hurt?"

David pointed to his shoulder. She graciously complied by kissing his shoulder.

"And it hurts here." David rested his hand on his chin.

Her eyes sparkling, she gave him a peck on the proper area.

Trying to hide his grin, he gave her his best pitiful look. "Thank you, but one more thing, my pride." Taking a chance and hopeful, he pointed to his lips. "And here."

She slid a step closer, wrapped her arms around his waist, and pulled him toward her.

Lost in the wonder of her sweet embrace, he kissed her again and again.

When David finally stumbled out her door or more floated out her door, if that was okay for a guy to think about floating, but what else could he say? He was smitten.

He'd never felt this way about anyone. His family loved her, and maybe he didn't know all there was to know about Marie, but he wanted to keep seeing her, take care of her, and, God willing, one day make her his wife. Was it too soon to think that way?

He shouldn't rush and needed to take his time. Granddad would tell him to pray. Right. David nodded to himself. He needed to pray, so he prayed as he walked to his car.

Stopping, he stifled a chuckle. He knew his begging prayers to keep Marie in his life and make her his wife sounded more like a little kid asking, please, Daddy, can I keep her, please?

Of course, the adult thing, the proper thing to pray, would be to ask for God's best for all concerned. He needed God's perfect will for him and for Marie.

David buckled in his car and drove to his house. He wanted to be the right man for Marie and the right man in God's eyes. To do that, he needed a cold shower and lots and lots and lots of prayer.

Chapter 19

After double-checking the numbers, Marie finished her report and stood by the printer waiting for the job to finish.

Yesterday had been amazing. She loved David's family, and if she was honest with herself, she was falling in love with him. She was willing to take the risk and see where their relationship went, but the big question remained . . . would she have to move again?

"Hey."

Marie jerked at Alexa's sudden appearance beside her. Not that she should be surprised, but how Alexa moved that fast remained a mystery.

"Tony called." Alexa grinned as she made a little dance move.

"Really?" Marie would have paid to listen in on that conversation. "Do tell. What did he say?"

"Not much. I talked, he answered yes or no, along with an occasional grunt or gasp."

Marie chuckled. She could just picture Tony all wide-eyed as her friend chatted away. "So, is that promising?"

Alexa propped her backside on Marie's desk. "We have a date this weekend."

"Great."

Alexa shook her head, "No, not great."

"What? Why? I thought you wanted to date him."

"I do, of course, but the thrill of the chase, the hunt, may be over." Alexa placed the back of her hand on her forehead, all dramatic-like.

"You've got to be kidding. You haven't even been out on one date. The chase is on, the hunt is not over."

Alexa stood and rubbed her hands together. "You're right. I have work to do. I need to decide on an outfit, get my hair trimmed, maybe even sharpen my nails, I mean, get a manicure." She zoomed down the hallway, leaving Marie with her mouth open. Poor Tony had no idea what awaited him.

"Hey," Alexa popped back in the door. "Don't forget lunch at 11:30. I'm driving so we can get there quicker."

Marie gave her a thumbs up and settled into her seat. She loved working and living here and spending time with David and his family. Maybe, as Joshua had told her, this move was more good than bad. She might not have had a storybook life, but she did have a crazy one. The truth was definitely stranger than fiction.

After a high-speed ride to town for lunch, Marie savored the great food.

"You spent time with David again and his family?" Alexa pointed her French fry toward Marie. "Girlfriend, this is sounding serious."

"It can't be serious." Marie shook her head. "I have been here that long, and we barely know one another." that she didn't want things to get serious with David. adopt David's family in a heartbeat or wished his family adopt her. And David's sweet personality and grea sure didn't hurt.

"My grandparents married after knowing one another for two weeks. " Alexa held up her fingers. "Yep, two weeks. But let's get back to the matter at hand. Marie, spill it. We want details."

Marie couldn't stop her smile as heat warmed her cheeks. "David's really nice."

"Ha, your expression says more than nice." Alexa glanced at Grace. "She's twitterpated."

"I see it." Grace nodded. "Love is in the air."

"Love?" Marie sat straight. "I can't be in love after only a few weeks."

"I thought we already covered that." Alexa leaned forward, her expression serious. "Time has no constraints when the love bug bites. Why would that even worry you? I say dive in and enjoy."

Marie picked at her food. "It's not that easy." She wished things were different or she could tell someone about what she was going through. No matter how she felt about David, she couldn't risk things going too far.

"*Au contraire*, my little friend," Alexa said. "Don't be one of those people who quote things like it's better to not love than have not lost."

Grace shook her head. "I don't think that's what you meant to say."

Alexa shrugged and waved her hand at her friend before turning back to Marie. "Don't be like the people looking back at their lives wishing they had taken a chance on love. Go for it. David's a nice guy, and his family is nice." Alexa's eyes narrowed. "Wait a minute, is that what's wrong? He's too nice? Are you one of those girls who only wants bad boys?"

"No, there were plenty of those where I grew up."

"That's a bummer. Sorry about that. But now you're here. Go have fun," Alexa said.

Grace nudged Marie. "Do you need our help? We could hogtie him for you so you can brand your mark on the boy."

"Hogtie and brand?" Marie shrunk back. "No, please."

Alexa shook her head. "Grace, you've got to stop reading those westerns."

"Maybe so, but things in the old west would have made this easier. Men were always looking for a good woman." Grace's eyebrows drew together as she gazed at Marie. "And, you're a good woman. Right?"

Marie nodded. "I think so."

"Okay, then I agree with Alexa, go for David. Dive in. I could maybe lasso him for you."

"You can lasso?" Marie surveyed quiet, shy, unassuming Grace. What else did she not know about her friends?

"She can," Alexa said. "She's been practicing. I had to stop her from roping the little dog we saw at the park the other day."

Grace crossed her arms. "I would have let him go. I wouldn't have hurt him."

"Maybe not, but the dog might have been traumatized."

Grace sighed. "Kill joy."

"Hello, ladies." Grinning, David stood by their table.

Marie glanced up at him as a steady heat warmed her cheeks. "Hi, David."

"We were just talking about you," Alexa's mischievous smile said trouble was brewing.

"You were? Good, I hope."

"Oh, *very* good," Alexa smirked. "Want to join us?"

"Thanks, but I can't. We have a shipment of seafood coming in pretty soon."

"Seafood?" Marie grinned at him. "I may have to come by later to pick some up."

David smiled. "That'd be nice. I work late tonight."

"That's nice."

"Yeah, seeing you would even be nicer."

"Oh, my goodness." Alexa waved her hand at them. "Y'all are terrible at this. It's obvious he's gaga over you, and you're gaga over him. Stop the nice stuff, set up another date, and get it over with."

David stood looking momentarily stunned. He then leaned close to Marie's ear. "Want to go out Friday night?"

"That would be nice," she whispered.

He chuckled. "Good." Straightening, he looked at the others with a grin. "This weekend, we have a date."

"It's about time," Alexa muttered. "Saves you from being lassoed, hogtied, and branded."

David's face paled, and he stepped back. "I better get back to the safety of the store."

Alexa laughed as he practically ran out of the restaurant.

"Maybe we should go easy on him," Grace said. "He might not be able to handle all the attention."

"Don't be ridiculous. What guy doesn't love attention? At least he made a move." Alexa slid her gaze toward Marie.

"Looks like things are moving forward. Do you need us to chaperone?"

A pent-up chuckle escaped Marie as she shook her head. Even though that would be entertaining, the last thing she needed was the two of them making snide remarks or hogtieing poor David. "No, I think we'll do just fine."

Alexa let out a long sigh. "Well, you know where we are if you need us."

Incredibly impressed, David surveyed Marie's handiwork. How did he get so lucky to date such a gorgeous woman with an amazing skill set? "I can't believe you know how to do plumbing." Their Friday night date had gone great, and now here she was, helping him with his remodeling projects. Even though he'd balked at her spending Saturday morning working with him around his house, she'd convinced him it was something she'd enjoy.

Marie turned on the faucet and glanced at David. "One of my many skills."

"You're like a jack of all trades. Super beautiful and super handy." He stepped toward her and took her in his arms. Marie melted into his embrace. Loving the feel of her closeness, he rested his chin on the top of her head.

"Hey, anybody home?" The front door opened, and Tony's voice carried from the entry hall.

"We're in here." David gave Marie a quick kiss and stepped back. Heat crawled up his neck at her cute grin.

Tony and Alexa walked toward them. From the look on their faces, their date last night must have also gone well.

"What you doing?" Alexa grinned as she glanced back and forth between them.

David waved his hand toward the amazing woman he had the privilege of actually dating. "Marie replaced the faucets in the bathrooms and kitchen."

"You da woman." Alexa gave Marie a fist bump. "I'm impressed, want to get a pizza with us?"

Marie gave David a curious glance.

"Thanks for the invite," David shook his head, "but I've already got dinner in the oven."

"Really? You cooked?" Alexa cut her eyes toward David.

"Yes, I can cook. Okay, actually, my mom made us something, but I had to warm it up."

"Well, you'll miss the best pizza in the area," Tony said. "Plus, we're going to see that new spy movie."

"Spy movie?" He loved spy movies.

Tony stepped toward him. A knowing grin on his mustached face. "The action movie where the hero stops the bad guys from taking over the world. Kinda like the Bond movies."

Oh, man. He didn't want to miss that one. David turned to Marie. "Want to go?"

"Sure, but what about your dinner in the oven?"

"Oh, yeah, I guess we'll pass." But then again, why couldn't they go? He could always save the food for later. "No, wait. I'll put it in the fridge."

After a great movie, the aroma of garlic and baking pizza

made David's mouth salivate as a waiter led them to a booth in the restaurant.

"I want to be like the hero." Tony settled next to Alexa across from them. "Dashing, tough, and can take anything thrown at him."

"You're my hero." Alexa squeezed his bicep and leaned against him.

"Aw, shucks." Tony's face flamed beat red.

David inwardly groaned. He still couldn't believe those two were dating. "It would be nice to be a hero," David nodded toward Tony. "But, I'd hate to leave my family like the guy in the movie, but if it was to keep them safe, I guess I'd do it."

"I'd do it," Tony said. "But I'd figure out how to stay in touch. You know, like some code-type thing."

"A code would be good. A lady on television used to tug on her ear to signal her grandmother all was well."

Tony shook his head. "We couldn't go on TV if we were being hunted."

"Good point." David sat back and rubbed his chin. "It'd have to be something obscure, out of the limelight. No social media. Mailing something would be a problem. I wonder what Sherlock Holmes would do?"

Alexa glanced at them both. "Not sure about Sherlock, but I'm not close to my family, so no problem. No need to worry about codes and stuff like that. Just get on with my life."

David turned to Marie. "What about you?"

"Me?" She adjusted the napkin on her lap and kept her head down. "You do what you have to do."

"Yeah, I guess so." Her comment almost seemed personal. What was in her past that kept her so guarded and secretive? Hopefully, as they got to know one another better, she would trust him enough to share.

"The movie made a big mistake," Alexa said. "In the scene in the mountain cave, I counted the shots he fired. His magazine would have been empty before he finished shooting."

"How can you be sure?" Tony asked. "Maybe his gun held more than you knew."

"No, it's obvious he wasn't using a 33-round big stick magazine. It was a stock Glock 19, four-inch barrel with a double-stacked fifteen-round magazine, and I would assume one was in the chamber."

Marie gave her friend a thumbs up. "It's one of those plastic fantastics."

David turned toward her. "What?" How did she know that?

She grinned and lifted her chin. "The gun frame is made of a reinforced polymer, reducing the weight and increasing durability. Corrosion-free, it absorbs recoil and is easy to maintain. And the black surface minimizes light reflection, which is an advantage in tactical circumstances."

Alexa nodded. "I can field strip one of those things with a blindfold over my eyes. My dad was in one of those alphabet agencies," Alexa waved her hand as though she'd mentioned nothing unusual. "You know, one of those CIA, NCIS, FBI, ABC things."

Tony leaned toward Alexa. "Man, I love you."

Alexa gazed his way, and a slow grin played across her face. "Really?"

Face, flaming red, Tony's eyes rounded to saucers. "I mean, wow. Um, that's cool. About the gun, you know. Uh, um ...." He grabbed and chugged his water, then choked.

Alexa patted his back. She didn't comment, just smiled as the poor guy continued to sputter.

Hoping to diffuse the situation for Tony, David passed a desperate look toward Marie. "How about you? How did you know about guns?"

She gave a slight shrug. "I told you. I grew up in an interesting neighborhood."

David squeezed her hand. "I hope you find good, interesting things here."

Happy and content, Marie floated to her kitchen for a glass of water. David's goodbye on her front porch left her with enough kisses and hugs to make her believe life had turned around and she'd finally found home.

Marie stopped in her tracks. Did she hear something?

A whimpering and scratching sound came from the back porch. *Filbert?* Did he come for a visit, or was something wrong with Mr. Doss?

Looking for her furry friend, she stepped outside.

An excruciating jolt knocked her to the floor. Her scream locked in her throat.

Chapter 20

Burning, agonizing convulsions shook Marie's body.

"A taser sure does come in handy." Max, his speech slurred, sat on top of her, holding her on the ground. "You didn't think I'd come unprepared against someone with a black belt, did you?" His hair disheveled, and his face unshaven, he reeked of alcohol.

His bloodshot eyes surveyed her as he leaned close to her face. "It's because of *you* I lost my job. Because of *you*, I can't get a job in this area. Stupid small town where everybody knows your business. Because of *you*, I will probably have to move. And I just bought a place on the beach last year. You're going to pay for what you took from me." He raised his fist. "I'm going to mess up that pretty little face of yours so no one will look at you again. But first, I'm going to have a little fun." His gaze roamed over her body.

Immobilized by the taser and Max, she prayed desperately for help. But help wouldn't come. *Oh, God. Please help*. Tears ran down her face and filled her ears.

A quiet movement came from behind Max.

Thwack!

Max slumped against her, then rolled off with a groan.

Mr. Doss, cane in hand, stood over Max, then turned his tender gaze toward her. "I'm sorry I didn't get here sooner.

And I'm sorry I didn't hit him much harder."

A sob broke from her as he helped her off the floor and wrapped her gently in his arms. Unsteady on her feet, nauseous and disoriented, Marie leaned against him as he helped her to the couch.

"Filbert was upset and barking. I knew something was wrong when I saw the car parked in your driveway."

Max groaned but didn't move. Mr. Doss hurried over and knocked the taser away with his cane. Standing over her assailant, he called the police.

Her life had finally turned around, and now this. Would she *ever* have a quiet, safe year where nothing terrible, weird, or life-altering happened?

The following hours passed in a blur as the police came and took her statement. The Chief, his eyes filled with kindness, peppered her with questions as Mr. Doss sat beside her.

Max, cursing and stumbling, had been handcuffed and led away. The Chief promised charges would be filed against Max and he wouldn't bother her again.

The Bowmans and even her backdoor neighbors, Maybelline and Chester Taylor had come over to check on her.

Mr. Bowman promised to install outdoor motion sensor lights on her patio and in the backyard. Everyone offered to stay with her and sleep on the couch and floor. Even Filbert seemed to want to stay by her side, but Marie didn't let them.

Locking herself inside, she set her alarm. She shuddered, thinking of what would have happened had Mr. Doss not come when he did.

Tears stung and blurred. Not again. She wouldn't cry again. She clenched her fists, tensing her muscles to will away emotion. Running to her bed, she took a pillow, placed it over her face, and screamed.

The opening music over, Marie tried to focus her tired eyes as she sat next to Mr. Doss at church. She needed answers and reassurance from God that life would get better. She wanted everything to go well this time, this one time. Was it too much to ask?

Why did God keep dangling something good in front of her, and then something terrible would happen? Didn't God care for her? She seemed to draw evil like a magnet.

The pastor came on stage. His eyes red as though he'd been crying, he paused and gazed at the congregation. "My long prayer list for others brings me to tears. I'm honored to pray, for they have shared their pain, trials, and heartaches. Several have incurable diseases and, with horrific pain, scream through the night. Yet, they continue to honor and praise God, secure in the knowledge one day they will be cured, whether here or when they are safe in God's arms."

Grief evident on his face, he swallowed hard. "Others have pain from the past that has left scars inside and out. External wounds have healed, but emotional pain remains. Messages, e-mails, and private conversations, share details of sorrow and pain, keeping my heart tender and full. I pray for their healing. I tuck their sorrow and pain into the pockets of my heart, and I carry their concerns to God. I pray for each one and pray for words to say to show them that God's love is real and that He cares. Each tear cried is precious to God, and He gently tucks them into His precious heart."

The pastor paused and opened his Bible. "Psalm fifty-six, verse eight reminds us that God has taken account of our wanderings. He's put our tears in His bottle and written them in His book." His gaze rose to scan the audience. "God knows every tear you've cried, each fear you face, every heartache, all your painful moments, and He cares, and His love never ends. And one day when this life is over, and health is restored, justice is served, and sadness replaced with joy, we will be enveloped safe, forever loved in the pocket of God's heart."

Marie sat still, spellbound, as the pastor continued sharing story after story of people who had faced difficulties and yet found God's love, faithfulness, redemption, and restoration.

Did God really care that much? Did he know every tear she'd cried, all the times she'd been afraid, scared, and alone? If only she could climb into the pocket of God's heart and be kept safe forever.

After the service ended, Mr. Doss walked with her as they stepped outside.

David ran toward them. "I heard what happened. Marie, I'm sorry. Are you okay?" He took her in his arms and held her tight—his heartbeat racing. "I should have stayed with you longer. I'm so sorry I wasn't there."

"It's not your fault. Max would have waited until you left, no matter what time."

David didn't let her go. "Want to come to lunch with us?"

"I'm not sure about being around too many people right now." Even though she loved being with his family, she needed something quieter.

"Okay. Can I just take you somewhere, maybe pick up something to eat, and go to the lake house or beach?"

She nodded. "Maybe the beach."

Mr. Doss patted her shoulder. "I'll be praying for you."

During the drive, they didn't talk much. David seemed to know she needed time to process everything that happened.

He parked his car in the driveway of a two-story beach house, then turned toward her. "Family friends own the place, and we're always welcome to use their private beach."

They left their shoes in the car. David grabbed towels from his trunk as she carried the meal they'd picked up through a drive-through on the way over.

A mild breeze offset the warm temperature. David continued to give her space as they sat on the blanket and ate in comfortable silence. The sound of gentle waves almost lulled her to sleep.

Two seagulls landed a few feet away from them and crept closer.

David waved the birds away. "If you're done with your lunch, I'll put the trash in the car to keep it safe from the seagull patrol."

When he left, Marie rose to her feet and stepped into the ocean, letting the gentle waves lap at her ankles. The ocean made her feel so small, insignificant, just a speck in the cosmos of life.

David returned and stood next to her. "Have you ever thought about God tucking us into the pockets of his heart? It's hard to understand how much God loves us, isn't it?"

"Yes." Marie turned toward him. "I believe God loves me, but there's this little doubt that he really does."

His expression held tenderness as he surveyed her. "Is it difficult because of all the bad things you've gone through?"

She nodded. "It's like the waves, crashing over and over. There'll be a quiet moment, then something else will happen."

"I'm sorry. You've had more than your fair share of troubles."

If only he knew the truth. She shrugged. "My grandmother used to say life isn't fair, but God is good. It's hard to understand if God is loving why bad things happen."

"Most of us would prefer an easy life and be happy, wealthy, and wise."

"That would be nice."

"Yeah. We can be honest with God about the terrible things that happen. Jesus said we'd have trouble in this world but to take heart because he's overcome the world."

"I wish he'd overcome my trouble."

David squeezed her hand. "Maybe Jesus said to take heart because we're tucked into God's enormous, beyond comprehension, loving heart. It doesn't mean it's easy and, at times, will be painful, but nothing can touch our souls. We're eternally safe in God's heart forever."

Marie stared at the ocean. "I just wish God's pocket was

zipped closed to keep out the bad things."

"Yeah, me too. I guess that's when we get to heaven." David took her in his arms and held her against his chest. "Marie Delgado, you are forever tucked into my heart."

Chapter 21

Sensing she was being watched, Marie glanced up from her work computer.

"Are you okay?" Alexa leaned forward and placed her hands on Marie's desk. "You should have called."

Grace nodded. "I have a buddy who works with the state police."

"I appreciate that," Marie said." I really do. It's over." At least she hoped the situation with Max was over.

"I knew Max was a jerk, but what he did is awful. I heard Mr. Doss split Max's head with a baseball bat, and his dog attacked him."

Marie couldn't help but grin at that visual. "It was a cane, and little Filbert did growl."

"Rats. I like the bat idea better and imagining a pit bull."

"Sorry to burst your bubble. The police did take Max away with enough charges; he shouldn't come back around."

"Well, he better not. We've put out an AP with B on him."

"All points bulletin?"

"No. Apprehend perp with bat." Alexa rammed a fist into her other hand.

Marie choked back a laugh. "Well, I hope for Max's sake he stays away."

Grace, her eyes full of concern, came around the desk

and knelt before Marie. "Seriously, is there anything we can do?"

"Thanks. I'm okay. But maybe a taser of my own would come in handy."

Alexa gave an approving nod.

"If you ever want to talk, just call one or both of us, okay? We're here for you." Grace hugged her. "Night or day, call."

Marie's throat too tight to talk, she nodded.

Alexa also gave her a quick hug. "If you want us to come over and stay with you, or you want to come over and stay with us some night, we'll have a slumber party. I'll wear my lightning bolt pajamas. They even have feet in them with track shoes."

Marie chuckled. "I just might take you up on that sometime."

After her friends left, Marie stared out her window. Despite all that had happened, she was grateful to be in Crawdad Beach, where people seemed to care about her. Maybe she was tucked into God's heart after all.

Even David said she was tucked in his heart. She hurried to finish her work so she could see him and let him know he was definitely tucked into hers.

David swept up the shrapnel from the toddler who had broken into a bag of cookies. Fortunately, the mortified and apologetic mother had bought three bags before she left.

If only he could sweep away Marie's troubles. Hadn't she

been through enough? He only knew a tiny part of her past, but the thing with Max made his blood boil. She'd said she grew up in a rough neighborhood, but how rough was it that she needed to be a black belt and knew about guns?

He'd been sheltered growing up in Crawdad Beach, he just wished he could shelter Marie now.

"David?" Brenda, wearing a low-cut blouse showing way too much cleavage, walked toward him. "I need your help."

Surprised to see her on her day off, David nodded. "Sure. What's the problem?"

"Well, If it's okay with you, I'd like to take off work tomorrow." She stepped closer and laid her hand on his arm. "I hope that won't be a problem. It's just that something came up, and I need the day."

David took a small step back, creating a more comfortable space between them as he mentally reviewed tomorrow's schedule. He would again be shorthanded. He needed to hire someone more reliable. "Brenda, this is the fourth time you've taken extra days this month."

"I know. I'm so sorry. It's just that..." She sniffed and put her hand over her mouth, but no tears formed. Batting her eyelashes at him, her pitiful look didn't look very pitiful, just rehearsed.

"Brenda, I'll have to move you to temporary status if this continues."

"What?" She glared at him as she put her hands on her hips. "I work hard when I'm here."

"I appreciate your hard work when you are here. But you're not here very much lately."

"Well, I'll have to think about this. I need a job where I can come and go whenever I want."

"Okay. Well, maybe we should discuss what would work best for you."

"Maybe so." She stepped toward him and tripped.

He grabbed her before she face-planted.

She smushed her body against him and smiled in way that he knew she'd done that on purpose. "I knew I could count on you."

He disentangled himself from her clutches. "Let's schedule a time to discuss your employment status when my father is here."

Brenda huffed. "Fine. I still need off tomorrow. My boyfriend is in town."

Marie hurried out of the store. She thought David was different, but she'd seen the curvy blonde in his arms. He was like the rest, making her believe he was a good guy.

Hot tears blurred her vision as she drove to her place. How could she be so stupid? She slammed her fist against the steering wheel. Hadn't she learned anything over the years? She should never have let her heart be vulnerable.

Inside her place, she threw her purse on her couch. She hated emotions that made her feel weak. Standing rigid, she clenched her fists as the wounds from her past flooded into her consciousness. The memory of the guys in her old neighborhood who'd befriended her and only tried to use her.

The other times, she'd had to fight to keep somewhat unscathed by the evil that lived around them.

Sick to her stomach, she fell to her knees. Emotion bubbled as grief poured out. Things would never change. She'd always have to fight for her life, live on the run, and never have a safe place.

The sound of knocking at her door pulled her attention. She forced down the emotions, willed herself to stuff them, swiped away the tears. She couldn't afford to be weak. No one would help her.

The knocking grew louder. "Marie? It's David. Are you home?"

She ignored him.

"Your garage door is open, and I can see your car. Are you okay?"

She let out a growl. How stupid that she'd forgotten to close it. Maybe he would think she went for a walk.

"Marie?" David's voice grew frantic. "Are you okay?" He pounded on the door.

"Go away."

"Are you okay? Marie, please let me in." He pounded again.

"Go away!"

"I'm not leaving."

Her cell phone rang. David's number showed on her screen. He wasn't going to leave. Might as well get it over with. Tell him to leave her alone. She didn't need anyone's help. She'd made it on her own this far.

She opened the door, and David rushed toward her and

took her in his arms. "Man, I was so worried. Are you okay?" He stepped back and studied her face. "What's going on?"

She punched his chest. "I saw you with the blonde at your store." She spat the words at him. Hoping she wounded him as much as he did her.

"What?" Confusion crossed his face. Then his eyes went wide. "No, that was Brenda. She tripped and fell. I caught her. I'm *not* interested in her. I pushed her back. Didn't you see that?"

Marie shook her head. "No." Was he telling the truth? Had she assumed based on past experiences with other men? Deep down, she knew David was different. But still, he was a man.

He took her back in his arms and held her close. "Please trust me." With a gentle touch, he tilted her chin up and waited until she looked at him. "I love you, Marie."

He loved her? She swallowed hard as her anger melted away. David loved her? How could he? He didn't know all she'd been through and all she was going through.

"David, you barely know me."

He cradled her face in his hands. "I know enough to know I love you."

Could she believe him and take the risk of loving and being loved? How could anyone love her?

Her conscience pricked. What about God? Did God really have her tucked into the pocket of his heart? Did she trust him or not?

Why did she go back and forth feeling alone in the universe and yet wanting to believe God loved her? Why couldn't she rest, relax, and trust God? She silently prayed, asking God not to give up on her.

David held her close, resting his chin on her head. "I love you. I'm here for you, and I'm not going anywhere."

Marie nestled in his arms. She had to stop the past from ruining her future. It was time to trust God and trust the sweet guy God had put in her path. "I love you too."

Chapter 22

Six wonderful months. Marie looked across the white tablecloth at David as she finished the most fantastic meal and dessert she'd ever had. How could one man be so sweet, handsome, loving, and wonderful? He wasn't perfect, but he sure was close.

The time they'd been dating had flown by with long walks on the beach, jet skiing at the lake, doing fun projects at his house, and spending time with his family.

David grinned. "Give me a minute. I'll be right back."

Marie sighed and turned to look out the restaurant windows. The brilliant orange sun disappeared into the water, signaling day had turned to night. Soft music played in the background.

David returned a few minutes later, holding a wrapped gift bigger than a shoebox. Grinning like a little boy, he handed it to her.

"What's this? You shouldn't have gotten me anything."

"Just open it." David's eyes sparkled. "I hope you like it."

Marie carefully removed the bright red bow and the silver wrapping paper. She gasped.

Inside sat a little bear with a pocket in his heart. "Oh, David, this is so sweet." She picked up the soft, plush animal and held it against her chest. "Thank you. I'll keep it forever."

"I hope so. Marie, I love you." He got up from his seat and went down on one knee.

Marie sucked in a breath. He was going to propose?

"Marie Delgado, will you give me the pleasure and honor of being my wife?" He opened a little velvet box with a sparkling diamond ring inside.

Tears blurring in her eyes, she let out a happy squeal.

Movement in her peripheral vision drew her attention. Over David's shoulder, a dark-haired man stood watching them. Icy tentacles of fear snaked down her spine. He looked too much like the killer.

The man glared at her, then turned and walked away. She let out a breath. Even if it weren't the man, she could not, would not endanger David and his family.

"I can't, David. I love you so much, but I can't." Pushing back from the table, she grabbed her purse and ran out of the restaurant.

She could never place David and his family in harm's way. Shivering in the night air, she stood beside his car. Ramming her fists into her eyes, she tried to stop the tears.

Hands gently tugged against her forearm. "Why? Tell me why? Is it me?" David's anguished face gazed at her.

"No, it's not you."

"Is it something in your past?"

She nodded.

"Marie, whatever is worrying you. The past is over, and I don't care what happened. We have now, today, and the future. I want you to be my wife."

"I want that too, but I can't." Why couldn't she throw all

her fears in the air, grab him by the arm, and run away from life? Why did she ever let her heart fall in love when her past might kill her, David, or his family? She shook her head. "I just can't."

He held her against him. "Please." His voice broke.

"You don't understand. The past might be over, but my past follows me, and my past can kill. I can't take that chance. I love you, and I love you all too much. I just can't. Please take me home."

Her tears spent; Marie curled up on her couch. David had left her at the front door without even a good night kiss and just walked away. He looked so hurt, so miserable. She knew the feeling.

She'd ruined her dream come true. Her past had destroyed her future, shriveling her heart, her hopes, and her dreams.

A soft knock came from her front door. She didn't want to move, but maybe it was David. Rising to her feet, she plodded forward. Every movement seemed like being underwater—slow and laborious.

Mr. Doss stood on her porch.

As soon as she opened the door, he wrapped her in a fatherly hug. "David told me." His deep voice reverberated in his chest. "Would you be willing to share what's going on? I know you love David."

She collapsed on the couch and pulled a throw pillow to her chest.

He sat next to her. "Marie, whatever you decide, you will

always be loved by us all."

She was so tired of hiding, being alone, and not telling anyone what she'd been through and was still going through. If she could trust anyone, it would be Mr. Doss.

Marie took a deep breath and let it out. Through teary eyes, she told him about her parents being killed, being raised by her grandmother in a lousy neighborhood, witnessing the murder, being taken into protective custody, moving to New Mexico, and then to Crawdad Beach. She spilled it all, all the sordid details. She just let it out. "I don't know how long before my life is again in danger, and I couldn't live with myself if something happened to one of you."

Mr. Doss took her hand and waited until she raised her watery gaze to his. "Marie, I am very sorry for all you have been through. Hopefully, the authorities will soon catch that man. But none of us has guarantees in our lives. Only God knows the number of our days. I truly believe God brought you here for a reason. David loves you, and I believe you love him too. My family loves you."

Her lips trembled, and her eyes swam with fresh tears.

Mr. Doss gave her hand a tender pat. "I will keep a more diligent watch on you, and I can pray for your protection and ours. Regardless of what might happen, you can stop running."

How could she be loved by this man, David, and his family? "What if the killer finds me? What if that puts you all at risk?"

"Marie, I believe God brought you here for us, not just for you. We've been praying for years for David, a good,

Godly wife, to bless him and our family. Before you were born, God knew exactly what would happen and when. Even though you've been through many hardships, you have survived; you've gone *through* those hardships. God promises all things work for the good for those who love him and are called according to his purpose. You belong to God, you have a purpose, and He will turn your past, present, and future into a beautiful ending."

His tender eyes held her steady. "None of us has any guarantees we won't be put in harm's way, but what happens to me and my family is under God's sovereignty. Please don't shut out David or the rest of us. You've been given an opportunity for a new beginning."

Marie drew in a calming breath. Telling Mr. Doss felt like a burden had been lifted off her shoulders, but should she tell David? Could she take the risk with her heart and with his?

Mr. Doss stood, stepped toward the door, then turned toward her. "One other thing. Please read the story of Ruth in the Bible. She lost all she knew in her old life, but God blessed her with a new home and family."

After he left, she sat on the couch and opened her grandmother's Bible to the book of Ruth. Marie read how God cared for her, blessing her in ways she probably couldn't have imagined.

She looked up at the ceiling. Would God be kind enough to do the same for her? If only God would give her a sign. She loved David and loved his family. She believed they also loved her.

Could she trust God enough with her and David's future

to say yes? But what if he didn't want to ask her again? Did she completely blow her chances with him?

She fell to her knees and prayed long, hard, and pleading prayers for God to show her what to do and what was right.

A knock on her door brought her to her feet. Maybe Mr. Doss came back to say something else.

Marie peeked through the peephole. David stood on her front porch. She fisted her hand on her mouth. Did she have another chance? She'd beg and plead if she had to for him to take her back.

Opening the door, she let him inside.

David drew her against his chest. "I'm not going to let you get away. I believe God brought you here. And I believe God brought us together."

She held him tight. "I don't want to lose you."

"You didn't. You won't. I'm not going to let you go." He stepped back and went down on his knee. "Marry me." He held out the box with the ring to her again. "I don't know what's going on. But I won't let you get away without telling me why. You do love me, don't you?"

She nodded. "Yes, I love you, but before I accept the ring, I need to know if you can accept something about me."

"Nothing you can say will make me change my mind. I love you."

"You say that now, but when I tell you, you might not think it's worth it."

"It won't matter."

"Stand up, please." Marie removed her contacts, looking at him through her original gray eye color. "I'm not who you think I am."

He stood and grinned. "Cool, you have gray eyes. They're beautiful. Just like you."

"It's not just that. I wasn't born with this name. I'm in protective custody because I witnessed the murder of a major drug kingpin a few years ago."

David's eyes rounded. "*That* murder?"

She nodded.

"Wow. Okay. Witness protection, huh?" Emotions flitted across his face. "You're not Marie Delgado?"

She shrugged. "Not originally."

"Well, okay. Do I need to know your other name?"

"Angelina."

"Angelina. Oh, I like that. But, I guess I need to keep calling you Marie."

She nodded. "I've been as honest as I could without telling you everything. I haven't been married or have an ex-boyfriend somewhere. It's just me. David, if something happens, I might have to move again."

David rubbed his neck for a few minutes. "Okay. If it does, I'd go with you. Nothing you can say or not say makes a difference. I love you." He took her hands in his. "Marie, where you go, I will go. My family will be your family. We have the same God, and he will guide, direct, and keep us safe."

Marie sucked in a breath. Was that her sign? That was almost what Ruth had told her mother-in-law before they journeyed together. Marie closed her eyes and said a silent prayer. Would God be so very kind to give her what she'd always wanted?

"Marie Delgado, or whatever your real name was, will you be my wife?"

David knew about her and still loved her. "Yes!"

Enjoying her Saturday morning, snuggled in a warm blanket, Marie sipped hot coffee as she sat on her back porch. The month had flown by as they planned to be married in a private ceremony at their church with David, his family, and a few of their friends.

Just last week, his family gave her a wonderful engagement shower in their home, giving them fun and practical items to start their lives together. And, in two weeks, she would be David's wife. Her smile might not ever leave.

Her cell phone buzzed, and David's picture came on her screen.

She grinned as she answered. "Hiya, you hunk of a man." The statement usually got a chuckle out of him.

"I'm on my way over." His voice sounded upset.

Marie sat straight. "Is everything okay?"

"I hope so. I really hope so. I'm turning down your street right now." The call disconnected.

Marie hurried to the door as David's car pulled into the driveway. He rushed toward her, shut the door behind him, and handed her the local paper. "Our picture is on page fifteen and is also online. My out-of-town cousin thought she was doing a favor for us. She didn't know. I'm so sorry."

Head swimming, Marie took the paper. Sure enough, a picture of them at the engagement party with their names, where they lived, even the date they were to be married.

What if the killer saw them? What if he came after her and David and his family?

"Maybe it'll be okay." David held her tight. "I've already called the paper and had them remove it from their website. Maybe no one out of the area saw it."

Marie blinked away the burn in her eyes. "What if he did see it? What are we going to do?"

"It's going to be okay." His statement didn't sound all that positive.

She drew back. "Your cousin didn't place the announcement anywhere else, did she?"

"I don't know. I don't think so. I'll call her." He punched in the number and walked away.

Marie's lip trembled. Not now. How could this happen? Why? What if he found her? What if she had to move again?

His shoulders slumped; David walked toward her. "She didn't notify other papers, but she did put our photo on her social sites, and she's very, very social."

Marie bit her lip, tried not to cry. "Oh, David. What are we going to do?"

"Let's not panic. God brought us together, so he will take care of us."

"Yes, but sometimes God works in ways we don't understand. You know that. All through the Bible, bad things happen to people."

"But God gets them through the bad things."

"Yeah, and sometimes getting through them means getting to heaven."

David pulled her into his arms. "It's going to be okay." His words sounded soothing, but his heart pounded in his chest.

The church service over, David scanned the crowd, then hurried toward his grandad standing in the church lobby. "Have you seen Marie this morning?"

"No, I was wondering if she was here."

"I haven't seen her, and she's not answering her phone."

His grandad pointed with his cane. "We need to check on her. I'll meet you there."

David drove as fast as he could without putting himself or others in danger. He'd spent Saturday with Marie, and she seemed calm when he left that night. But still, he'd barely slept as he prayed desperate prayers for protection.

He parked in her driveway and peeked in the top windows of her garage door. Good. Her car was there. Maybe she just wasn't feeling well. He knocked on the door and waited.

His grandad hurried toward him and peered through the front windows. "Is she home? Knock harder. I can't see much of anything."

"Her car is in the garage." David knocked again. "Maybe she's on the patio." He ran to the back of her duplex. She wasn't there either.

If something happened to her, what would he do? He

looked through the French doors. The light over her table was on, and the ring box sat with a piece of paper leaning against it. "Oh, God. No. Please, no."

He sprinted to the front, to the Bowman's door, and pounded. "Please, I need your help."

Julie Bowman answered. "Is everything okay?"

"I don't know. Please, can you let us in to check on Marie?"

She glanced back and forth between David and Mr. Doss. "Sure. I know you both love her. Dustin, can you hurry and get the key to Marie's place?"

Dustin, with key in hand, ran out the door. "Did something happen? You don't think it's Max again, do you?"

"We're not sure, but please check. Her car's still in the garage, but she's not answering. She wasn't at church this morning, and she's not answering her cell."

Dustin unlocked the door and stepped aside.

"Marie?" David rushed in, running from room to room. She wasn't there. The only things that seemed to be missing were her grandmother's Bible and the little bear he'd given her.

He ran to the table and picked up the note.

I love you, David. I will always love you. I can't risk you or your family being hurt. Your love will forever safely be tucked into the pocket of my heart.

Heart shattering, he sank to his knees. "Noooooooooooooooooo!"

Chapter 23

Numb, dead inside, Marie held the little bear David had given her against her chest.

She'd just gotten ready for church when Joshua had showed up at her door telling her Mr. Smith said it was time to go, they were moving her again. Since they'd seen the photo, Mr. Smith didn't want anything happening to her.

Not wanting David or his family at risk, she'd left with Joshua.

She stared at the road in front of them. Was running again the answer? Why did she just jump in the car because Mr. Smith wanted her to go? She'd been moved from place to place by someone she didn't even know. What was she thinking? She had a great life in Crawdad Beach. Why did she leave?

"Joshua, tell me about Mr. Smith."

He glanced her way. "What do you want to know?"

"Everything. I've been trusting him, but I don't know him. I don't even know you. How do I know who you really are?"

"You're right. It's time." Joshua slowed the car, pulled into a gas station, parked, and turned toward her. "Mr. Smith's actual name is Smith Chatman. He was part of a covert military team your dad had been on that eliminated a vicious terrorist. In the raid, several sons who worked in the terrorist organization had also been neutralized. However, the youngest son, Diab, was attending college in the States. He vowed revenge on anyone who had been on that team. When he found out Smith had been the leader, he killed Smith's wife." Joshua took a deep breath and slowly blew it out. "Diab is the one who killed your parents. When Diab ran your parent's car off the road, Smith was able to save you but not your parents. He took you to your maternal grandmother's house and has been watching over you ever since."

Marie gasped. Smith's wife and her parents had been murdered?

"I was also on the team," Joshua continued. "Your father was a great guy, Marie. We've all tried to keep you safe. Diab didn't know you survived until your name and photo ran in the paper when you were promoted at your job in California. That's how he found you and why he tried to kill you in the coffee shop."

"Diab is after me? But, I thought I was in protective custody because of what I saw that day."

"You are in Smith's care because of who you are. He knew Diab had found you. That's why you were taken to New Mexico. Diab found you again when the company you worked for placed employee photos online. And now, your engagement photo was online. We can't risk losing you."

Marie rubbed her forehead and tried to make sense of everything Joshua was telling her. "So, I've been in the government witness protection?"

"No, you've been under private protection through Smith's firm. After serving in the military, he opened his enhanced security company."

"He's been paying all this time to protect me? How could he spend all that money and time?"

"Smith was best friends with your dad," Joshua said. "He even introduced your mom to your dad. He feels responsible for you because your like family."

"Why didn't he just tell me? Why couldn't I have known who he was and what he was doing.?"

"He didn't want you to put you at greater risk. The less Diab knows about your connections, the better."

Marie shook her head. Even with all she now knew, she didn't want to keep running. "Joshua, I appreciate all Smith has done for me, but I don't want to leave the family I've been given now. I don't want to live on the run for the rest of my life. Please take me back to Crawdad Beach. Call Smith and thank him for me, but I want to go home. I've found home, and I want to go back."

His gaze studied her for a moment before he gave her a nod. "I'll take you. Give me a minute, and I'll make the call." He stepped out of the car.

Marie silently prayed for help and wisdom as she watched Joshua talking on his phone. She knew it was risky, but even if she only had a few weeks with David and his family, it would be better than a lifetime on the run.

Joshua slid back into his seat. "Smith doesn't like it, but he understands. You know, you might have seen Smith around town. He lives in your area."

"What? Really?"

"You don't have a picture of him, do you?"

Joshua scrolled through the photos on his phone and

184

handed it to her.

"I know who he is. He waved when I drove into Crawdad Beach, and I saw him at Tiddlywinks restaurant. And I think I've seen him other places around town."

"If you saw Smith, he wanted you to see him. He's been watching over you since you were a baby." He pulled the vehicle back on the road, back toward Crawdad Beach.

Marie rubbed her eyes as flashes of memories went through her mind. When she was a little girl, someone grabbed her arm, keeping her from falling in front of a moving car. Another time, several guys in a local gang had walked toward her, then turned and ran. And when she looked behind her, a man was walking away. Even at the coffee shop, when Diab tried to shoot her, a man who looked like Smith had run after him. She hadn't noticed until she thought back.

Joshua glanced her way. "Smith has been there in person for you many times, but I know he has prayed for you every single day. Even if you choose to stop his protection, you have someone who loves you and will never leave or forsake you." He pointed up. "Marie, I know you haven't had an easy life, but I believe God has great plans for you. Someday, your story will help many, many people. Let's get you home."

A few hours later, Marie thanked Joshua and stepped out of the car. Since she'd left her keys in the duplex, she ran to the Bowman's door and knocked.

Julie answered and threw her arms around her. "You're safe!"

Marie chuckled. "Yes. I'm safe, but I don't have my key."

"We were so worried about you." Julie stepped back and

looked at her like she'd been gone for years. "Are you okay?"

Marie nodded. "Yes, someday, I'll explain, but right now, could you let me in so I can grab my car keys."

"Yes, sure. David and Mr. Doss were here earlier, and they were so worried about you. David was sobbing when he read a note."

"Oh no! I've got to find him." Marie ran to her place, grabbed her car keys, and drove to David's house. He wasn't home. She hurried to the store and checked his office. He wasn't there. She ran from aisle to aisle, looking, hoping, and praying.

A hand vice-gripped her arm as a cold, blunt object jabbed her in the back. "Don't say anything. Just walk with me out of the store."

Diab? Her heart slammed against her chest; every muscle tensed. This could not be happening. Not now. Not when she was trying to finally get a happy-ever-after with David.

Molten lava flowed through her veins as she contemplated her next move. There was *no* way this man would ruin the life she'd now been given. She could use her martial arts skills against the man if she could just get into position.

A young woman with a baby in the cart came their way.

"Don't do anything stupid," the man's voice hissed. The object dug harder into her back.

Marie curbed her thoughts and stared straight ahead. She couldn't take a chance on trying anything with other people around. Maybe when they got outside, she could do something.

Sending up silent prayers for help, she walked methodically toward the door. As soon as they reached the threshold, she would make her move. Each step she counted in her head.

Five....

Four....

Still heartsick and sick to his stomach, David wandered through the store. He'd been praying and begging God for answers, for his help. Why did Marie run? He had told her he would go with her, but she'd left without him. Maybe she didn't love him after all.

He turned the corner and stopped. *Marie?* Walking away from where he stood, her posture ramrod straight, Marie walked next to a man. His hand, covered by a jacket, was against her back as they moved toward the door.

Was that the guy who had been after her? No way he was going to lose Marie again. David glanced around, looking for a weapon. He grabbed a can of tomato sauce.

With a prayer that his throwing arm and wrist were still strong, he aimed for the man's head and let the can fly.

Thwump!

Unconscious, the man crumpled at Marie's feet.

Chapter 24

"**S**mells wonderful."

"Thanks, Grandad." Marie turned to face Mr. Doss. "Spaghetti should be ready in about fifteen minutes." Having him move in last year had been a blessing. David's mom had built an addition onto their house to give him a private bedroom and den, and his delightful presence was a joy to them all.

Filbert nudged her with his nose, hopeful that some tidbit of food might come his way.

"Celebrating the anniversary?" Grandad grinned.

Marie held up the dented tomato sauce can. "Four years ago today." Who would have thought God would use something like that to stop a killer. Even though the experience had been terrifying, the family still laughed at David's choice of weapon to take down the bad guy.

Marie handed Grandad the spoon. "Would you mind stirring the sauce for a few minutes? I think David is the one who needs to be rescued right now." Grabbing her jacket, she stepped out on the back deck.

David circled the backyard, followed by their two children and their little dog, Filbertina.

In dramatic, slow motion, David collapsed on the ground. "You're just too fast for me." Feigning exhaustion, he moaned.

Their son and daughter, giggling with glee, piled on his back.

"Mommy, we caught him!" Angelina's face glowed with happiness.

"I got him too!" Smith playfully punched David's back.

"Good job kids! You might need to give Daddy kisses to get him back on his feet."

Both kids squealed as they planted slobbery kisses on their dad.

"Dinner's almost ready. Help daddy get up and go wash your hands." Smiling, Marie returned inside. She never would have thought her life would be like this. Happy, safe, and blessed with a sweet husband, three-year-old twins, and a wonderful family.

When she returned to the kitchen, Grandad relinquished his stirring duties to her. "It's a good life, isn't it Marie."

Marie nodded. "Yes, it is." She leaned against the kitchen counter. God had blessed her in more ways than she could imagine, even using her terrible past to encourage others when she shared her story.

And the best part? All this time, she had been visible yet hidden safe in the pockets of God's heart.

The End

Dear Reader

Thank you for reading *Hidden, yet Visible*. Although the characters are fictional, most of us have encountered hardships and difficulties. I created Crawdad Beach as a safe place for Marie. I hope you enjoyed the quirky and sweet characters as much as I did. Lord willing, I plan on continuing the series. (Please visit the last page to view some fun crawdad artwork by Jack Foster).

Crawdad Beach, South Carolina, doesn't really exist; however, God has blessed with an eternal safe place through the sacrifice of His Son, Jesus Christ. God demonstrated His love toward us in that Christ died for us while we were still sinners. For God so loved the world, He gave His only Son so that everyone who believes in Him will not perish but have eternal life. (Romans 5:8, John 3:16).

As I wrote the letter from Abuela to Marie, I thought of us all. God has given precious promises to help along our journey.

Therefore, this letter is for you...

God created you, weaving you together in your mother's womb (Psalm 139:13). He knows the plans He has for you, plans for your future to give you hope and peace (Jeremiah 29:11). God's love is unfailing and eternal. He will never leave you or forsake you (Hebrews 13:5), and no one can snatch you out of the hands of Jesus or our Father God (John 10:28-29).

God's steadfast love never ceases; His mercies never end; they are new every morning, and His faithfulness is so very great (Lamentations 3:22-23).

I pray that the eyes of your heart may be enlightened so that you will know the hope of His calling (Ephesians 1:18). For you are God's workmanship, His own master work, a work of art, created in Christ Jesus for good works which God prepared for you beforehand so that you would walk in them, living the good life which He prearranged and made ready for you (Ephesians 2:1.).

Call on God in your day of trouble, and He will rescue you (Psalm 50:15). Be strong and let your heart take courage (Psalm 31:24). Don't worry about anything; instead, pray about everything. Tell God your needs, and don't forget to thank Him for His answers, and God's peace will be with you. His peace is far more wonderful than our human minds can understand and will keep your thoughts and your heart quiet and at rest as you trust in Christ Jesus (Philippians 4:6- 7).

Christ gives His peace not like the world's peace -- His peace, so don't let your heart be troubled or fearful (John 14:27). There will be trouble in the world, but be courageous because Christ has overcome the world (John 16:33).

Trust the Lord with all your heart, and don't lean on your own understanding. In all your ways, acknowledge Him, and He will make your paths straight (Proverbs 3:5-6). Delight yourself in the Lord, and He will give you the desires of your heart (Psalm 37:4).

Whatever you do, whatever your task may be, work from

the soul, putting forth your very best effort as something done for the Lord and not for people (Colossians 3:23).

Don't ponder the things of the past God will do something new. He will make a way through the wilderness and streams in the desert (Isaiah 43:18-19). Wherever God sends you, remember Jeremiah 29:7 to seek the peace of the city where God has taken you and pray to the Lord for it; for in its peace, you will have peace.

People can do terrible things, but God will punish those who do wrong (Colossians 3:25). Trust in God, and don't be afraid of people because the Lord is for you (Psalm 56:11, Psalm 118:6). Be strong and courageous, don't be afraid or discouraged for the Lord your God is with you wherever you go (Joshua 1:9).

Nothing can ever separate you from God's love -- not death, life, angels, demons, things present, things to come, no powers, nor height, depth, nor any other created thing will be able to separate you from God's unlimited love, which is in Christ Jesus our Lord (Romans 8:38-39), for nothing is impossible with God (Luke 1:37).

When you need a friend, remember that Jesus has called His followers His friends (John 15:15). He is always with you (Matthew 28:20). He is a Father to the fatherless, and He even puts the lonely in families (Psalm 68:5-6).

When your heart is breaking, remember that the Lord is near the brokenhearted, and He saves those who are crushed in spirit (Psalm 34:18). He heals the brokenhearted and gently binds up their wounds (Psalm 147:3).

God grants the desires of those who fear Him; He hears

their cries for help and rescues them (Psalm 145:19).

So please always love the Lord your God with all your heart, soul, and mind. (Matthew 22:37).

You are forever safe in the tender pockets of God's loving heart.

Acknowledgments

My precious Savior, Jesus Christ, thank You for saving me and being a safe place for every heart that comes to You.

My sweet husband, thank you for your support, encouragement, help, and fun suggestions. I love you!

Bonnie Engstrom, thank you for your feedback and encouragement.

Cathy Brewer, thank you for the many hours of listening and helping me as the story unfolded.

Jack Foster, thank you for the fun crawdad artwork.

Readers, thank you for reading. You all have blessed me. Thank you!

About the Author

Lisa Buffaloe is a happily married mom, multi-published author, and speaker. When Lisa's not writing, she enjoys gardening, walking with her husband, and exploring God's beautiful nature.

Visit Lisa @ https://lisabuffaloe.com

Books by Lisa

Fiction
Visible, yet Hidden
The Masterpiece Beneath
Nadia's Hope
Prodigal Nights
Writing Her Heart
The Discovery Chapter
Open Lens
The Fortune
Grace for the Char-Baked

Non-Fiction
Float by Faith
Heart and Soul Medication
Time with The Timeless One
The Forgotten Resting Place
Present in His Presence
We Were Meant for Paradise
One Lit Step: Devotions for your journey
The Unnamed Devotional

Flying on His Wings
Unfailing Treasures
No Wound Too Deep For The Deep Love of Christ
Living Joyfully Free Devotional (Volumes 1 & 2)

Crawdad fun

Jack Foster, thank you for the cute drawings!

Thank you for reading,

Visible,

yet Hidden

Made in United States
Orlando, FL
08 November 2023

38642973R00113